"I'm sorry my parenting skills aren't up to par."

Kylee crossed her arms over her chest. "I told you my only experience was with interns. Maybe if there were penalties for the twins' behavior, they would follow orders."

"What are you going to do? Fine them?" Evan quipped. He held firmly to Annabelle's hand as she began to tug. "Demote them?"

"Funny," snapped Kylee. "If Mia had—"

She cut herself short just as a fist of pain struck Evan's chest. "You have no idea how Mia raised her children," he said in a low tone. "You weren't around."

"Well, I'm here now." Kylee's retort sounded confident and challenging, but her mouth drooped as lightning flashed in her eyes.

"I'm here to help you, Kylee."

"Why don't you take them on home for lunch then, and I'll be right behind you."

"Fine," said Evan. "I'm sure they would rather read anyway."

"Enjoy your time with them. I'm going to get a cupcake."

Her tone sounded smug. *His* time with them.

His time with them was running short.

T0188688

Danielle Thorne is a Southern girl who treasures home and family. Besides books, she loves travel, history, cookies and naps. She's eternally thankful for the women she calls friends. Danielle is the author of over a dozen novels with elements of romance, adventure and faith. You'll often find her in the mountains or at the beach. She currently lives south of Atlanta with her sweetheart of thirty years and two cats.

Books by Danielle Thorne

Love Inspired

Visit the Author Profile page at LoveInspired.com for more titles.

A Guardian Till Christmas

DANIELLE THORNE

LOVE INSPIRED

INSPIRATIONAL ROMANCE

LOVE INSPIRED®

INSPIRATIONAL ROMANCE

Recycling programs
for this product may
not exist in your area.

ISBN-13: 978-1-335-93686-8

A Guardian Till Christmas

Copyright © 2024 by Danielle Thorne

Love Inspired
22 Adelaide St. West, 41st Floor
Toronto, Ontario M5H 4E3, Canada
www.LoveInspired.com

Printed in Lithuania

MIX
Paper | Supporting
responsible forestry
FSC® C021394

And all they that heard it wondered at those things which were told them... But Mary kept all these things, and pondered them in her heart.
—*Luke* 2:18–19

To my readers, friends and family.
May the Light and Life of the world be your true star
and guide you home.

Chapter One

Kylee Spokes adjusted her designer sunglasses, stepped out of the taxi and broke off the heel of her shoe. She gasped as pain shot to her ankle—but it was more for the high heel. The driver fetched her bags from the trunk while she picked up the heel and limped into the browning grass of her sister's front yard, relieved she'd brought a spare pair.

"Have a good day!" the driver called.

Kylee waved as he drove off, imagining him laughing at her for singing to the radio when a favorite song from high school played. That'd been almost two decades ago, which made it an oldie now. She shuddered at the thought.

Lugging her suitcases behind her, she hobbled up a sidewalk dotted with autumn leaves and colored chalk graffiti. "What a mess," she mumbled as she eyeballed the small single-story cottage that had belonged to her sister, Mia, and her husband, Chip. For a fleeting moment, Kylee felt a tug of emotion over being home, then she remembered they were gone and this was only a temporary stay. But her life as she knew it was over.

The small spark of contentment faded like the lawn. There was an upside-down riding toy at the bottom of the porch stairs and a suspicious-looking handprint on the railing. Kylee whimpered, looked down at her wool skirt and slid out of her suit jacket. The turquoise silk cami underneath it had cost less and would clean up easier. She took a deep breath and braced herself for adorability and the noise, mess and guilt complex that came with it.

The doorknob turned easily, and she left her luggage on the small square porch and walked inside.

"Mom, I'm here!" she called.

She kicked off her other high heel and looked around. The open living and kitchen space was empty. It was quiet down the narrow hall, too. Curious, Kylee dropped her purse and sunglasses on the narrow island, noting there were no dishes in the sink. Her stomach shrank at the sign that Mia was no longer around, and their mother kept things shipshape now.

The front bedroom was a cracker box that only had room for a computer desk and a small sofa. Kylee pushed open the bathroom door and saw plastic toy boats overturned in the bottom of the tub.

The next room belonged to the twins. Henry's cars were all over the floor, and Annabelle's stuffed animals were piled on the bottom twin bunk. There were no children in here. That left Mia's bedroom.

Kylee couldn't bring herself to look inside, knowing it was crammed with her late sister's things. Mom had asked her to sort them out when she found time because she hadn't been able to do it. *Post-funeral duties.* Kylee frowned. That, on top of figuring out what to do with a set of twins she was now in charge of. How had it already been three months?

She pushed open the back screen door. The warm Georgia sky looked royal blue over trees that had shed half of their orange-and-red leaves for November. Her mother was nowhere in sight, but there were little legs draped over one of the hammocks in the yard. The other hammock was full, too, but as motionless as a mummy.

Kylee tiptoed over to the skinny legs stained with red clay and green bruises. "Boo!" she shouted playfully.

Henry and Annabelle shrieked and sat up, then erupted into gales of laughter. "Aunt Kylee?" Henry blustered, as if he wasn't sure he recognized her.

Ignoring the stab of guilt for not being here since the funeral, Kylee wrapped her arms around the kids just as the other hammock spun like a centrifuge, and a big, heavy body fell out and hit the ground.

"Hey!" cried the familiar-looking man lying in the grass.

She didn't know whether to gasp or burst into laughter along with the children. Kylee let go of her niece and nephew and straightened.

The man scrambled to his feet like he was going to karate chop somebody with his thick arms then stopped. "Oh, hey, you're…"

Kylee cocked her head. It was Evan Hollister, Mia and Chip's friend, acting like a guard dog. Besides vague recognition from perhaps the funeral, she'd seen pictures of him and knew that they thought he was great. "I didn't mean to startle you. Where's my mother?"

The man crossed two muscled arms over his chest. "You're Kylee." He stood his ground like she was an invader. "I'm Evan Hollister. We met at the funeral service."

"That's right," said Kylee, pretending she remembered that day when really it was all a nightmarish haze of tears and guilt. "You're helping with the twins. You're Chip's best friend."

"Was," Evan stated in a stoic tone.

"Yes, he mentioned you a few times," Kylee replied. "I'm sorry. Chip Maxwell was like a brother to me."

"As he should have been."

Kylee threw daggers with her stare to cover the pang his words caused. She hadn't been close to her brother-in-law because working as a creative director for a big social media company in New York hadn't allowed them to get to know each other well. "Is my mom here?" she repeated.

"She comes over before dinnertime," Evan said as if she should know.

"Aunt Kylee," whispered Annabelle.

Kylee looked down to find her niece hanging on her leg and peering up at her with her brilliant blue eyes. "What's the matter, princess?"

"I'm hungry."

"Have you had lunch?" She looked back at Evan. "If my mother's not here, who's minding the children?"

"I am." He frowned. "And they've had lunch. It's almost dinnertime."

Kylee glanced at her watch and realized four-year-olds probably didn't do late lunches. She turned to Annabelle. "Baby, come inside, Auntie Kylee will give you the treats she brought you from New York."

Annabelle shot Evan a grin, but he gave her a stern look. "Go wash up inside, and we'll have reading time first."

"Yay!" cried the little girl. "Henry, it's time for candy!"

Kylee didn't miss Evan's frown.

"Good," said the dark blond little boy who matched his sister. He dangled his chin over the edge of the hammock. "I hate rest time."

"It's good for you," said Evan. "But it's over. Now, books."

"Okay," Annabelle surrendered in an agreeable tone.

Kylee raised her brows in surprise. "You don't want candy?"

"Yes." The little girl stole a look at Evan.

"After reading time," Evan countered, ending the discussion.

Kylee started it right back up. "We'll have books *and* candy," she announced, and both children dashed toward the house. She turned to Evan. "Mom informed me you'd be helping out. Thanks for keeping an eye on them, but I'm here now. You can go."

Evan took three steps and stopped short of Kylee's toes. "We're on chapter three of *Charlotte's Web*. I'll hang around until after your mother gets here like I always do."

"You do this every day?" Kylee wondered if the burly, gray-eyed man was a librarian.

"I've taken over for your mother," Evan informed her. "She asked me to help with days, and she sleeps over at night."

"Well, I'm here now until I take them to New York." Kylee tried to cover her confusion by looking confident. When had Evan Hollister been made guardian of Mia's children?

"I'm also the twins' godfather," he reminded her.

"I'm their aunt, and the children have been left to me because my mom thinks she's too old to parent again." Kylee lifted her chin.

"Your mother has fibromyalgia."

"There are nannies, and she's stronger than you think," she responded.

Evan gave her a penetrating stare. "Henry and Annabelle need family, not nannies, and your mom has been ordered to take it easy. That's why I've stepped in."

Was Mom worse? Why hadn't she asked for help? "I'm family," she said at last. "And I plan to accept permanent guardianship of the children as Mia requested in her will.

I just needed some time before I could come down and deal with it."

"Evan," shrieked Annabelle from the back door. "We're ready to read the spider book."

Evan gave Kylee a parting smirk and brushed past her.

She prickled at the contact, then pulled up her hair, feeling the tiny hairs on her nape beginning to frizz in the Georgia humidity. The back door slammed shut, and she realized her niece and nephew had forgotten her. "I am family," she muttered again, although she didn't feel like it. In fact, thanks to Evan, she was the one who felt like the intruder.

Mrs. Spokes's voice was a welcome sound when she traipsed into the house and called, "Evan! I'm here!"

He sighed with relief. Reading to the kids was his favorite activity, but today had been uncomfortable because Mia's older sister was in the next room. Evan tried to pretend the cultured, attractive woman wasn't listening to his character voices, but it was hard. How someone like her could be related to the Spokes family he didn't understand, and why she took after her elegant, brown-eyed mother when she was nothing like her was a mystery. She'd insisted on giving the twins their candy first, and it'd taken a half hour to get them to calm down enough to read to them.

"We're in here," Evan answered from the twins' room.

"Nanna!" Annabelle forgot about Charlotte the spider and darted out. Henry flopped over and picked up a puzzle piece.

Evan followed Annabelle to the kitchen, where Mrs. Spokes gave them both a warm smile. A small grocery bag sat on the counter. "We were just finishing a chapter," Evan explained.

"That's wonderful." Mrs. Spokes pointed at the bag. "Thank you, Evan. That's less I have to do, not that I mind reading to them." Her thin arm looked unsteady as she lifted a can of tuna out of the bag. "I'm going to try to do more than a can of soup tonight for these kids."

"I'm sure they'll appreciate it," Evan assured her.

"Aunt Kylee brought us candy!" chirped Annabelle.

Mrs. Spokes set down the tuna. "She's here?"

"Yes." Annabelle grinned. She held up a hideous troll doll that lip-synched to Bluetooth music streams.

"Yes, she's here," agreed Evan. "She's unpacking her things in the office."

"Oh, wonderful. I'm so glad." Mrs. Spokes sighed.

Evan couldn't help but notice a glint of relief in her eyes and wondered if she realized her eldest daughter's arrival had put a hiccup in the twins' routine. Kylee was supposed to take over custody of the children, but she had no intention of raising them as Mia and Chip wished if she'd brought sweets and talking toys. Mia had been strict about how much candy the twins could eat, and Chip preferred toys that offered some type of STEM benefit.

Evan's nerves twinged. He'd been right to talk to his lawyer, Martin Tanner, about whether or not he should consider petitioning for custody. He'd promised himself when he failed to save his friends that he would see their twins raised safely. But according to Mrs. Spokes, Kylee planned to take them to New York at Christmas unless he could stop her. "I'm not sure about the toys she brought," he began, trying to be cryptic.

"Why not?"

He whirled around. Kylee stood behind him with Henry on her back. The boy tugged on one of her earrings tangled in her glossy, straight chocolate-brown hair. "Ow." She winced.

"Kylee!" Mrs. Spokes opened her arms.

Evan watched Mia's sister set down her nephew and pat her mother's back in a stiff gesture. "Mom," she muttered.

When they parted, Mrs. Spokes dragged her over to the groceries. "I brought fixings for tuna fish casserole. You can make that, right? Did you get settled?"

"I put my things in the office," Kylee replied.

"Oh," said Mrs. Spokes in a sudden halting voice. "I should have made up Mia and Chip's bed for you. I'm sorry."

Evan thought he saw Kylee shudder. "The sleeper sofa is fine," she insisted.

Her mother looked at her doubtfully. "If you're sure."

"Here." Kylee picked up the other ugly troll doll from the counter and handed it to Henry. He laughed and skipped away. "I haven't made tuna casserole in a while, Mom," she admitted with a wary glance at Evan.

He took the bait. "I can make it. I know going to the grocery store wore you out, Mrs. Spokes."

The older lady waved him off. "Angie Coles showed me how to make an order on my phone, and they brought it to the car."

"On your phone?" Evan repeated in surprise. Running into friends at Brook's Grocery was his favorite part of going to the store, but he could understand why Mrs. Spokes would use a delivery service.

"It's just easier," Mrs. Spokes admitted. "Isn't technology wonderful?"

"It is," exclaimed Kylee. "Children's toys are something else these days." She shot Evan an indecipherable look before marching to the counter to pick up a bag of egg noodles and scan the back.

"It's not that hard," Mrs. Spokes encouraged her.

"I know it's not," declared Kylee. "I'm just refreshing my memory."

"Just don't walk away from the noodles while they're boiling because the water goes away, remember?"

"I know, Mom."

"Do you need help?" Evan couldn't keep his amusement out of his voice. What girl from small town Lagrasse, Georgia, didn't know how to boil a pot of noodles? Clearly, Miss Kylee Spokes.

"No, I do not," Kylee responded curtly.

"Evan has to get to work anyway." Mrs. Spokes shook a finger at him. "I don't want you to be late at the station again because of us."

"Station?" repeated Kylee.

"I'm a firefighter paramedic. Friday night shift."

As if she'd heard it before, Kylee mumbled, "Oh, right." Surely she knew that he'd been the first to arrive at the scene of Chip and Mia's accident. Firefighter paramedics fought fires and handled medical emergencies. Sometimes, he reached a scene first.

Evan tried to act nonchalant, although he wanted to make the stupid tuna casserole and just be late. "They'd understand," he assured Mrs. Spokes.

Kylee put her back to him, but Mrs. Spokes set a hand on his arm in a gentle touch. "Thank you for all you're doing for us. We appreciate it, don't we, Kylee?"

"Sure," said Kylee without turning around.

Mrs. Spokes beamed like Kylee had sung his praises, and Evan couldn't resist giving her a quick squeeze like he would hug his own mother. "I'm glad to do it. The twins are family." He winked at her.

Mrs. Spokes grinned. "You'll have your own brood someday. You just need to get those night shifts changed and quit sleeping through the weekends when you're not with them. Enjoy yourself."

Evan knew Mrs. Spokes was right. He couldn't date on night shifts, not that he'd found anyone worth his time since Michelle had given up on him. Had it already been two years since they broke up? His heart twinged with the old hurt and disappointment. At this rate, he'd never have a family of his own. "It's been my honor to help," he told Mrs. Spokes. "They needed to be in their own home, and I am their godfather."

"I agree." Mrs. Spokes's smile was faint, the pain of losing her youngest daughter just beneath the surface.

Evan glanced at Kylee. The woman was fumbling with a can opener as if she'd never held one before. "Well, their Aunt Kylee is responsible for them now, so we're both off the hook for the day to day."

"Not until it's official," interjected Kylee. "I'll get that taken care of as soon as possible, but my lawyer said it could take up to eight weeks or more."

"Hopefully it won't take as long as it took you to get down here," said Evan.

She spun about as if he'd insulted her. He'd meant no offense. It just came out wrong. "It's not easy to leave a job just like that," she retorted. "Some of us have commitments."

"But you're here now," said Mrs. Spokes. "Mia and Chip loved and trusted you both, and I'm sure you'll be wonderful influences on these children. I couldn't rest easy with anyone else taking care of my grandbabies."

"Don't worry, Mom," Kylee reassured her. "I'll have everything in order in no time."

Evan bristled as if she'd hinted that he was incapable. Everything *was* in order, as much as it could be for two young children who'd lost both their parents. They were just beginning to act like they understood. Sarcasm was on the tip of his tongue, but he resisted, saying, "I'll get on to work now," and headed for the door. He paused, realizing that tomorrow's schedule was up in the air, the new life and routine he'd carved out the past few months in question. "So shall I come over in the mornings as usual or later in the afternoon?" he called to Mrs. Spokes from over his shoulder.

"Neither," replied Kylee. "If I need you, I'll call."

She might as well have ripped off a bandage. Maybe he *should* give Martin a ring and ask what it would take to get custody of the twins for himself. "Actually, since I'm still on the books as the emergency contact, I'll come over around Tuesday afternoon for reading time—and bring *healthy* snacks." He offered Kylee a tight smile when she sent him a hard stare, and he wondered how the arrangement with the kids would work out now with her here until Christmas.

Bolting out of the door before she said anything else, he backed his SUV out of the driveway.

He'd thought of Annabelle and Henry as family before their parents had died. He couldn't just turn them over to a… Well, their aunt was practically a stranger. She might be their legal guardian soon, but he wasn't going to abandon them to someone who couldn't be troubled to show up to her own sister's wedding; someone who attended her funeral in dark trendy sunglasses and then left before the wake.

He made a note to call Martin that night and let him know what was going on. He needed to keep the twins safe. Because in reality, the reason they were orphans was his fault.

Chapter Two

Kylee closed the children's bedroom door for the fifth time only to hear muffled giggling again. "I heard that," she called. "Go to sleep! You just lost another five minutes of TV time tomorrow."

There was a groan, and Annabelle shouted, "You're mean! I want to go to Ava's house!"

Kylee smiled to herself, despite the overwhelming frustration and having no idea who Ava was. She'd never babysat as a teenager because she could make real money waiting tables, and her lack of experience with kids showed. She swept several toy cars off the couch beside the small electric fireplace and collapsed.

The house smelled like burned cafeteria food. The kitchen table was covered with untouched plates of mushy noodles and stinky tuna, and the living room was a mess even though it had been pristine when she arrived. The invisible boulder she'd carried in her chest since her sister's car accident felt as heavy as a school bus.

Managing a staff of digital project managers is easier, she thought with a beleaguered sigh. And she had no cook or housekeeper here.

Mia had made the challenges of parenthood sound charming, but there'd been nothing fun about the past four hours. The twins didn't listen. They didn't follow directions. And they did nothing in a hurry unless it was something she told them *not* to do.

But the moment she heard of her sister's death, something had ripped deep in her core, accompanied by an explosion of guilt. She'd always meant to make up for not being there more for Mia. But impressing her parents—and Lagrasse—with a big-city career had taken precedence, and Mia had seemed happy without her. When Mom told her about the will and that Mia and Chip had requested Kylee raise the twins, she hadn't hesitated to agree. But it'd taken her some time to wrap her mind around it.

How could she handle two young children who didn't come with instructions? They were terrific in small doses, but the thought of managing anyone younger than an intern full-time was terrifying. She'd had a pet goldfish once. It only lived three days.

A weird cartoon shrieked from the television. Kylee knew Henry and Annabelle weren't supposed to watch more than two hours a day, but that was going to change. Besides, there was so much educational programming on television these days, it didn't matter. She'd read up on it. Cooking, however, she had not. That'd been evident when Henry whined for chicken noodle soup, then began asking where Nanna went and if Evan could come back. The tuna casserole was a disaster just as the man had implied it would be.

It would have been nice if her mother had informed her how much he'd been helping out since the funeral. When Kylee had confronted her, Mom had shrugged it off and said she hadn't wanted to bother her.

Kylee blew out a breath of frustration. Just thinking about Chip and Mia's friend made her nerves crackle. True, he was helping out during a horrible transition, but he was acting like he knew what was best, and it bugged her. He had the twins wrapped around his finger, and Mom acted like he'd hung the moon. He was apparently everyone's favorite now, just like Mia had been. It didn't seem to matter that Kylee had taken two months of leave from work before Christmas to pack up her sister's home and start raising her preschoolers.

The pity party skidded to a sudden stop. With a slow burn of embarrassment at her pride, Kylee remembered how Evan had read to the kids when he could have left. He'd offered to cook dinner, too. Really, he was doing the honorable thing stepping in with Mia and Chip gone, and he was gutsy for choosing to save lives as a paramedic. But although his solid, stocky physique suggested he could bench-press the school bus sitting on her chest, he was neither a Spokes nor a Maxwell.

She stared at the television, wondering what he thought about her. She was single, childless and close to forty with nothing to show for it except a hefty bank account and an enormous 401(k).

Most people in Lagrasse had probably written Kylee off because she'd chosen a high-powered career with a social media management company in the greatest city on earth, but she hadn't forgotten where she came from. She'd sacrificed a great deal so she could be successful—and stand out just as much as beautiful, popular Mia. Now they wanted her—needed her. Kylee had simply assumed she would have more time to resolve things with her sister, but she'd been wrong. Raising the twins was the only way to make things right, even if she had to give up the next fourteen years of her life to do so.

* * *

After a rather dull weekend off, Evan's night shift at the Lagrasse firehouse on the corner of Pine and Main began at 8:00 p.m. on Monday, and he found himself running short on time after staying too long at Murphy's Bookstore perusing new releases. He hurried back to his garage studio apartment to change, feeling out of sorts after not seeing the twins all weekend. Kylee hadn't even brought them to the Good Shepherd Church outside of Lagrasse where her mother attended and he'd joined since moving into town.

His landlords, the Lightfoots, were good Christian people who owned a majestic turn-of-the-century brick home with several windows that reflected the tree-lined street and sidewalks. Behind it, the separate garage was clean with whitewashed Hardie Plank and narrow stairs that led up to a second-story living space. They creaked under Evan's weight as he jogged up to the door, his mind distracted over the sudden changes at Chip and Mia's cottage.

Peppy, the Lightfoots' long-haired black-and-white cat, greeted him on the porch. He reached down and stroked her head as she rubbed against his shins then trotted down the stairs.

Evan pushed the door open and looked around for his uniform before remembering he'd left it in the dryer. After restarting the stacked laundry unit to fluff his crumpled clothes, he picked through the freezer for something to eat. There were two frozen dinners that wouldn't take long to cook, although the portions would only satisfy a snail. Dinner with the twins would have been more enjoyable.

Evan's stomach rumbled as he plopped down at his small dinette. He reached for his schedule to remind himself what he had going on the rest of the week besides midnight shifts Monday through Friday. As the microwave hummed, a small pebble of anxiety formed in his stomach. Except for sleeping, he had little to do on his days off besides visiting his mother thirty minutes away in the most rural part of the county. Most of his time the past few years had been spent at the bowling alley or at Chip's house. Since the accident, he'd quit the bowling league and found excuses not to go out with his friends from work or hang out with his family. He would have avoided church if it weren't for the twins because everyone who looked at him saw a man who'd witnessed the accident of one of the most beloved couples in town, and they knew he'd let them die.

The microwave beeped, and Evan exhaled to loosen the tightness in his chest. Without the twins to care for, he'd have a lot more free time, but what would he do with it? He wasn't sure. He wasn't ready to give them up, especially to Kylee with her designer sunglasses and citrus perfume. She made a pretty picture and smelled nice, but the second she started speaking he wanted to tell her to chill out. He already had a boss, and the chief worked at the firehouse.

Snorting, Evan shoveled the processed food into his mouth while ruminating over what to do about Henry and Annabelle. He couldn't give them over to a woman who didn't know how to boil noodles and had horrible taste in toys. Those troll dolls were sure to give the twins nightmares.

Checking the time, Evan realized he was going to be late again and dashed to grab his clothes from the dryer. He grabbed his keys, the new hardback book from Murphy's and the medical kit, then dashed out to the SUV he'd driven since high school. The gears ground as he zipped down the driveway, giving Mrs. Lightfoot a wave when she straightened from over her mums. The West Indian woman was a watercolor artist with a remarkable green thumb for perennials. She waved back with an arched brow, and he slowed as he turned out onto the street.

Work required him to be focused and clearheaded. He couldn't let another patient down; he'd walked through that dark valley already. He ignored the tasteless frozen dinner heaving in his stomach, but he couldn't erase Kylee Spokes from his brain no matter how hard he tried. She was the reason for his distracting day—another judge, another witness to his failure to save Chip and Mia—and she was taking the kids.

Evan took a deep breath and exhaled to release the stress raising his blood pressure. He wasn't going anywhere. No matter who Kylee was, he was staying in Henry and Annabelle's lives, and when she gave up and ran back to New York alone, all the better.

Evan turned into the drive of the brown brick firehouse and parked his truck around back. When he let himself in through the kitchen door, he inhaled the familiar pizza and diesel smells and relaxed. His partner, EMT Chase Anderson, and Captain James Noble were seated at a long, solidly built table waving sub sandwiches in the air while they talked with their mouths full. Shawna Lopez, another firefighter he enjoyed working with, was on her phone in the corner. Evan gave them all a nod and headed for the locker room to store his things.

"Hey, Hollister!" squawked Chase.

Evan strolled back out and took a seat at the table across from the gangly younger man.

"Did you hear about the Boggses last night?" Chase shook his head in disbelief, and there was amusement in his tone. "We got a call after nine in the evening."

Older and more serious, James grunted as he chewed his sandwich. "What happened?" Evan asked.

"Mr. Boggs stumbled and took a seat on the rug in the bathroom, then his wife almost fell into the bathtub trying to help him up."

Evan felt his eyes round with concern over the retired senior couple. "Are they okay?"

"Just a little bruised and sore." Chase waved him off, indifferent. "You should have heard them arguing like teenagers when we got there, though." He grinned.

"Last time we were there, I suggested they get some live-in help," Evan reminded them. "It could have been worse."

"We sent them both to the emergency room, and they checked out okay," said James. "Mr. Boggs was lucky he didn't break his hip. He was hurting pretty bad."

"Poor guy," sympathized Evan. "He's convinced he can still get around like when he was mayor."

Chase arched a blond eyebrow. "He was bellowing like an old heifer."

"You would, too, if you smacked your bones hard enough on an old tile floor," James scolded. "He's a good man. He was a great mayor."

"I'm glad he's okay," said Evan.

"He'll be fine," James mumbled. He reached for his sandwich but stopped before taking another bite. "How are the kids?"

"Funny you should ask." Evan leaned back, frustration bubbling to the surface now that he had ears to listen to him complain.

"Are they okay?" the captain asked in concern. He'd lost one of his own children who'd driven under the influence.

Evan let the front legs of the chair clap back down on the floor and leaned forward on his elbows.

"Their aunt arrived on Friday, the one from New York?

She turned everything upside down, so I stayed there until their grandmother got there."

"That's the big sister, right?" interrupted Chase. Evan nodded. "Is she as gorgeous as Mia was?"

Evan frowned at the question. He'd never thought of Mia as more than a good friend, and Chase was far too young to have known her in school. "If you mean attractive, yes."

"I remember her," said James. "Brunette, right? Tall? Not as fair?"

"Right, Kylee, with the beautiful brown eyes." Evan stopped short, surprised at himself. Why did he use *beautiful* and *Kylee* in the same sentence?

Chase gave a low, appreciative whistle.

Evan glared at him. "I wouldn't try that around her," he warned. "Kylee Spokes could pin you to the ground with the tip of her high-heeled shoe."

James choked out a blustering laugh, then wiped his mouth with a napkin. "She's high up in some New York company, isn't she?"

"I don't know the details, but I think it's Digital Rock, the social media company," said Evan.

"Wow, impressive," inserted Chase. "Especially for being from Lagrasse."

"Yes, she graduated from Lagrasse High School five years ahead of Mia, who was a year behind me."

"Did Chip know her?" asked James.

"I don't think they were close." Evan raised a tight shoulder. He knew they weren't.

"How'd she end up with the kids?" Chase wondered.

"Beats me," said Evan with a twinge of resentment. "Their grandmother has health issues, but I live here, and Lagrasse is all they know."

"She's family," said James, crumpling his wrapper. "I can see why Mia wanted it that way."

Evan clasped his hands tighter on the table. True, he wasn't related, but he was present and dependable. Also, he wasn't ashamed of his hometown and didn't need to dress like a Wall Street big shot to impress other people. "The twins know me," he insisted. "It's been three months, and we have our routine, and she's changing things around before she even takes them away."

"Kids are resilient," James assured him. "They'll be okay."

"I'm not sure she knows how to care for a child—or anyone else for that matter," Evan said. "She didn't know her mother's fibromyalgia had gotten worse—or she doesn't care."

"Maybe no one told her," suggested Chase. "She's probably busy with her career." His eyes glowed with admiration.

"Too busy to know what's going on with her family?" Evan growled. "I've never heard of her hanging around long for the holidays, either." He felt himself scowl. "I'm just going to keep an eye on things," he added in a determined tone. "Chip and Mia would want me to."

The two men across the table fell quiet, and Evan knew they were thinking of how he hadn't done enough for his friends at the accident scene, but he wouldn't let the twins down. He scooted back from the table with his book.

"I'm sure you'll do the best you can," called James. "It's good she's here now with the lieutenant's position opening up. You should apply."

"I don't know if I have time with the kids."

"They're going to be leaving at Christmas anyway, right? Maybe you can run by in the mornings just to see how she's doing. Let her know you're here to help until then."

Evan headed for the day room, leaving the unease behind him. He'd worked hard to make it to lieutenant, and it was so close. But then the accident happened. Could he work more hours and still be there for the twins? Was he even worthy? Kylee didn't make him feel that way. His friends couldn't possibly understand what he was talking about without meeting the intimidating woman. To make matters worse, Martin had left a voicemail telling him there was little to be done if the aunt had accepted custody. He'd have to prove her unfit.

The station alarm screeched, vibrating the walls of the firehouse. Evan dashed for the locker room. His feet felt like wings. Someone needed him. There was a life to save. For a few hours, he didn't have to worry about Kylee or the twins.

Tuesday morning, the world came into focus, and Kylee realized something was very wrong. Sprawled on the fold-out couch in Mia's tiny office, she looked up to see Annabelle grinning back at her. The four-year-old twin was straddling Kylee like a horse and had her arms pinned down at her sides as if she could actually hold her aunt down. She giggled.

"Annabelle, get off me."

"I'm *hunwry*."

Kylee raised her head a few inches. "Hun-*gry*. Now let me up. Please." She fumbled for her phone, pulled up the Reminders app and typed in Speech Therapist. Her eyes widened when she noticed the time, then Annabelle began to bounce up and down on her stomach. "Oof!"

The little girl laughed louder.

"Annabelle, let Aunt Kylee up, and she will find you a croissant."

"What's that?" the child asked as she slid off. Flopping

over onto the mattress, she began to make snow angels in the sheets, pulling the bottom one off.

"No, don't do that." Kylee sighed, but Annabelle rolled herself up like a mummy. "What are you doing awake?" Kylee grumbled as she crawled off the bed. "Don't kids sleep until noon these days?"

Annabelle began to sing as Kylee stomped to the bathroom. She usually never slept past six in the morning, but it was nine now. She still had jet lag, she decided, even though she had not changed time zones. Skipping church at the start of the week hadn't helped, although she'd had no intention of going with Mom anyway. The Good Shepherd congregation had a general sermon for everyone, then broke into separate Sunday School classes. It'd been a while since she'd gone at all so instead, she'd chased the kids all over and caught up on emails.

Kylee shut the door to the green-tiled bathroom, scowled at her messy hair and turned on the water to wash her face. She had raccoon eyes from her mascara proving she hadn't washed up well the night before. The door beside her thumped. "What?" she protested, splashing water on her face.

"I need to come in," said a tiny voice.

She sighed. "Just a minute, Henry."

"I need to come in *now*."

Now in four-year-old speak probably meant she was borderline too late. Kylee exhaled in surrender and pulled open the door to let the boy inside.

He gave her a stare, and she stepped out, smoothing down her hair with her hands. A loud bang in the kitchen made her pivot from the office instead of changing her clothes. She found a cooking pot rolling in circles on the floor.

Annabelle looked up at her wide-eyed. "I dropped it!"

"What are you doing?"

"Making grits."

"You know how to make grits?" Kylee shook her head in disbelief. "I'm thirty-eight, and I can't make them."

The dark blond child stared at her with innocent blue eyes, and Kylee picked up the pot and set it on the counter. "Go brush your teeth or something."

"I didn't eat anything."

"Well, go clean them first because I said so," said Kylee. There. That felt better.

Annabelle looked up in confusion. "I want grits."

"Sure, fine. We'll have something. What about cereal?" Kylee walked to the pantry realizing she should have taken inventory the night before, because they'd used up all the granola cereal during the weekend. And fast food had filled in the cracks. Now it was Monday. Major fail.

"We like grits and eggs," Henry informed her from the doorway. His hair was matted on one side, indicating he hadn't bothered to brush it during his takeover of the single bathroom.

Kylee swung open the pantry door and examined the narrow shelves. They were tidy enough but not in any kind of logical order. They were also full of...ingredients. She blinked in surprise. There wasn't any more cereal besides grits and a canister of oatmeal. Half a loaf of bread could provide toast, and there were three bags of different types of dried fruit, but there wasn't anything quick. Everything had to be mixed together and cooked in one way or another. She groaned in agony. "Don't you eat Cocoa Balls or anything?"

"What are those?" asked Henry from behind her. He seemed profoundly interested in the idea of something chocolate.

"I want grits," reiterated Annabelle. "Ava likes grits, too."

Kylee stared into the pantry again, hoping something would appear but nothing happened inside the cave of wonders. "Who has the time, and who's Ava?" she muttered.

"What's wrong with your hair?" queried Henry.

"Grits!" shouted Annabelle. She reached up onto the counter and lugged the pot back down and held it against her belly.

Kylee closed the pantry door in alarm. "I don't know how to make grits," she reminded her, then decided it wasn't anything to be ashamed of. "Grits are old-school." She scowled. "How about a smoothie?"

"Mom makes us smoothies," Henry admitted with some wistfulness, as if Mia hadn't been gone since August.

Kylee turned to the freezer. There weren't any premixed smoothie bags inside. "Do you have protein powder?"

"She uses bananas."

Used, thought Kylee, suddenly sad along with increasingly desperate. She looked around. There weren't any bananas on the counter, just two shrunken apples. "I don't know how to make a smoothie from scratch," she told Henry. She did not add that her interns usually picked them up when she wanted one from a coffee shop outside her office building. She sighed, realizing she still felt tired and wobbly despite oversleeping.

"I like scrambled eggs." Henry stared at her, but Kylee did not look back. She didn't know how to scramble eggs. Not without burning them.

"We'll go to Casey's Diner," she decided, remembering the restaurant where she hung out in high school. She was a guardian, not a personal chef. The children could have pancakes at the old diner that looked like a train car. They'd love it. It'd been sitting on the edge of town ever since she could remember.

"Pancakes!" Annabelle approved. She dropped the pot on the floor with a clatter and dashed down the hall.

"Do something with your hair!" Kylee called out. She turned to find Henry studying her. "What?"

"You have black eyes," he observed.

Kylee remembered the face that had looked back at her from the bathroom mirror. She groaned. It'd take an hour to make herself presentable, and it was almost ten o'clock. She couldn't go out in public. She was setting a bad example letting the twins see her like this. Resolved to set an alarm the next morning, she picked up the pot and set it back on the counter, hoping the four-year-olds could survive another hour without breakfast.

Suddenly the doorbell rang, and Henry raced to answer it before she could catch him. The sound of the faucet in the bathroom meant Annabelle was getting washed up, but the little girl yelped.

Kylee dashed down the hall. "Are you all right?"

Annabelle grinned at her from over the sink as she teetered on her step stool. "Yes." The faucet was on all the way and flowing fast.

The doorbell rang again. "Just a minute!" Flustered, Kylee ran for the door. At least Mom could cook. She'd know how to make grits and how to get the tangles out of Annabelle's hair. Henry was on his tiptoes trying to turn the dead bolt when Kylee reached the door. She flipped the lock and pulled it open.

"Evan!" Henry cried.

Kylee cringed. During their nightly phone call yesterday, Mom had promised to come by, and Evan was not supposed to worry about them anymore. Kylee pulled her shoulders back while Evan looked at her as if they hadn't just met a few days ago.

"Good morning…" he offered. It sounded like a question. He was wearing slacks and a dark blue shirt with badges from the local firehouse, and his short, neat hair was combed off to the side. He studied her with gray eyes that reminded her of forest mists.

"Aunt Kylee can't make eggs," Henry tattled.

Annabelle appeared dripping wet from her chin down to the middle of her pajama shirt. "I want grits!" she bellowed.

"Ah…" Kylee planted a hand on her hip. "I can make eggs," she said defiantly. *I just burn them.*

Evan nodded suspiciously like he was doing a welfare check. "Is everything okay here?"

"Of course. It's fine. I told you that you didn't have to worry about coming over." Kylee gave him a confident look. She had everything under control. Didn't she? It'd been four days, but it still felt new.

He looked past her. "Is that water running?"

"The sink is stuck," said Annabelle.

Kylee managed to keep her expression neutral. If she'd woken up earlier, she would have had the children dressed and fed. There was still candy in her purse…

"Oh, Annabelle." Evan sighed. He brushed past Kylee uninvited and charged down the hall.

She watched him go in irritation until his feet splashed into a puddle at the door to the bathroom. "Annabelle!" Kylee cried. By the time she caught up, Evan was inside twirling the faucet handles on the sink until they turned off. He reached for a stack of towels on the wall shelf.

"Here." He tossed one to Kylee, who found her bare feet in a pool of water on the tile floor. "She spins them all the way on and then gets confused how to turn them off."

"And plugs the sink?"

"She likes to watch it fill up. It makes a good swimming pool for her dolls."

"Great." Kylee plastered a smile on her face. "I guess I should have been watching closer." She squatted down and began wiping up the water on the floor. "I was in the kitchen making breakfast."

"Were you?"

"About to. Then we decided to go get pancakes at the old railroad diner."

"Um, that closed like three years ago."

Kylee grit her teeth to keep from moaning. "I didn't know that. I don't live here like you."

"Actually, I rent an apartment. My mother lives in my grandparents' farmhouse in the country."

"Oh. Has your father passed?"

"He's in Alaska. Haven't seen him since I was four," Evan said.

"That's... I'm sorry." Kylee breathed out as Henry appeared at the door. So Evan was used to being the man of the house.

"Evan, can you make us grits?" Henry pleaded.

"Sure, buddy."

"You don't have to do that," insisted Kylee.

"I don't mind." Evan crouched beside her and helped her blot the floor dry. He smelled faintly of soap and...pizza?

Her stomach grumbled. She winced in embarrassment. "You don't have any croissants on you, do you?"

"No. You'd have to go to The Last Re-Torte Bakery on Loger Street to find those." He straightened and hung the wet towel over the shower curtain rod. "But I do make grits, so let me get that started." He glanced at her and, before she could refuse again, said, "Why don't you clean up? I'll watch the twins."

Kylee looked down at herself. The bottoms of her silk pajama pants were wet. Her shirt was wrinkled from tossing and turning, and she'd lost a button somewhere. Quickly, she shut the bathroom door behind him.

If she were her own boss, she'd fire herself. Of course, no one else would have known she'd overslept if Evan hadn't come by. She hoped he didn't tell her mother. Kylee put her hands on the edges of the sink and watched the last of the water spiral down the drain. When she looked up into the mirror with a grumpy frown, it melted into a horrified stare. She'd forgotten about the state of her hair and the black smudges under her eyes.

Just great.

Chapter Three

Later, Evan stood at the stove and stirred the grits so they didn't stick, but really it was because he didn't want to get trapped into another small space beside Kylee. She'd spent over forty-five minutes getting changed, and he thought he'd heard her making phone calls, too. Just as he served the now-starving twins at the table, she wandered in and fumbled around in the cabinets.

He cleared his throat. "I made extra grits. You can warm them up with milk in the microwave tomorrow. Just stir them real good."

"You didn't have to do that."

"You say that a lot, but I don't want Henry and Annabelle to starve to death," he replied.

"They won't."

Evan slipped down beside Henry without mentioning the late hour and helped himself to a spoonful of grits with two fried eggs. "Yours are on the stove."

"Oh." Kylee turned around. "Thanks." Her hilariously smudged makeup had been cleaned off, and her tawny skin was glowing. The brown-black knot on the top of her head had been washed and allowed to dry in ripples down to her shoulders. Evan noticed it was not as straight as before and wondered if she usually ironed it out. She looked almost normal in a loose flowy blue blouse and fitted pants.

"You didn't have to make me breakfast." Kylee snagged his attention away from her attire.

"I know that." Evan gave her a serious stare so she didn't suspect his approval. "But I would have done it for anyone. It's called being polite."

She grimaced, or maybe it was a smile. He wasn't certain. "Thank you."

"I'm sure you're not used to having someone cook for you," he said.

She turned to the sink and filled a glass of water. "Oh, but I am. I have a personal chef who delivers my meals, and interns who get me smoothies whenever I need one." She put the cup of water to her lips and smiled. It looked like a challenge.

Evan tried to hide his disbelief. "I guess Mia was the cook in the family, then."

The smile flickered. "Yes, Mia was the cook. Cookies, cakes, casseroles, you name it. Another thing she was great at doing."

"Oh?"

Kylee hesitated, then shrugged as if it didn't matter. "You knew her. Softball, swimming, homecoming court. She was volunteer of the year at that animal shelter she helped out with during high school."

Evan studied her, then focused on his plate.

"I'll go to the store later and pick up some cereal for the kids," Kylee continued. "You don't have to come by every morning. We'll manage."

"Right." Evan saw how she was managing things.

Henry scraped his plate. "Honey, don't scratch the china," said Kylee. "Tell Evan thank you, Annabelle." Kylee clearly didn't want him here.

Annabelle climbed down from her seat, scurried over

and threw her arms around Evan's neck. Her sticky mouth brushed his shoulder when he leaned down to embrace her. "Thank you," she whispered in a sweet voice. "I love you, Evan."

"I love you, too," he assured her. He gave her a squeeze, and when he let her go, she hopped away like a rabbit.

"Thank you, Evan," said Henry. He was still working on the generous mound of grits he'd insisted he could eat.

Evan could feel Kylee's examination. It was nice of her to remind the kids to thank him, but he felt like he was being manipulated into leaving.

"I guess I'll head out and get some sleep," he said to the twins' aunt. Leaning against the counter, Kylee gave him a tight smile. "By the way," he added, "Mia never gave the kids anything processed. They don't eat sweetened cereal."

Kylee's dark eyes rounded in surprise. "Really? Well, they will now. We grew up on all the sugary, artificially colored cereal you could eat. That's how I got through college."

Evan chuckled. "Well, so did I, but I guess she had a change of heart. Kids will do that to you."

"I wouldn't know. I let my interns feed themselves," said Kylee airily.

Interns weren't children, Evan wanted to point out, but he didn't. He wondered if Kylee had ever truly been a kid. He bit down on a reply and headed for the door. "See you later, Henry and Annabelle!" he called, dismissing Kylee's scrutiny. He heard them holler back from their bedroom as he shut the door behind him.

He'd thought coming over to make sure things were okay might be an olive branch as James had suggested, but Kylee wasn't interested in sharing caretaking duties, nor did she appreciate any help in the kitchen.

That was too bad, he decided. The twins deserved better than going hungry all morning, so she was going to get help whether she wanted it or not. He'd be back.

The silky grits on Tuesday morning had been amazing. It was a good thing Kylee had taken her time over Evan's life-saving breakfast; not only had it reminded her of something she'd missed from home, it was the only time she'd been able to sit down all week because the twins ran around nonstop. The past three days hadn't been much better, although the fall temperatures were delightful. It was also nicer to look at the yellowing grass and emerald pines from a lawn chair than crowded city streets from a window. The birds made a more pleasant tune than car horns and growling engines.

One of the twins shrieked, and Kylee narrowed her eyes at the hammocks several feet away.

Nap time was a joke. How Evan settled the twins down, she couldn't begin to fathom. She had to separate them and sit in a lawn chair in the chilly shade, too exhausted to scold them anymore. Besides, if she got up, she'd have to start cleaning up the toys all over the yard, including the plastic kiddie swimming pool filled with brown foam. Annabelle had decided to help herself to the water hose and kitchen dish soap, and Henry had stirred dirt into it with a rusted garden rake.

"Stop it!" cried a childish voice, and Annabelle began howling.

With a grunt, Kylee forced herself out of her chair like a puppet being dragged by its strings. She marched over to the first hammock to find it empty. Annabelle had sneaked over to cozy up with her brother. Kylee glared down at them both.

Henry looked up in relief and pointed at his sister. "She keeps putting her finger in my ear."

Annabelle giggled.

"Please stop doing that, Annabelle," said Kylee. "You two are going to be too tired to function tonight."

"I don't need rest time," Henry insisted.

Kylee sighed. "Then go pick up your toys while I empty the mess you made in the kiddie pool."

The little boy and girl wrangled themselves out of the hammock with feigned obedience but loitered in the yard like a street gang. Kylee began issuing them assignments while tugging on the heavy pool.

Crunching the edges helped the icy water to flow out, but it sloshed down her shirt, pants and all over the pristine white sneakers she bought last summer. The edges of the pool scraped her forearms. Panting and heaving, she managed to get it over to the side of the house and drain it until it twisted weirdly and made a cracking sound.

"Great." She tossed it upside down onto the grass, wet and grungy. Then she scanned the yard to evaluate the twins' progress. Only half of the toys had been moved. Henry's sock drawer had been carried outside to find his most comfortable fit and was still upside down by the back door. The children were nowhere in sight.

Kylee felt a bellow building in her chest but took a deep breath, then exhaled slowly. She'd faced tougher situations with bigger and more powerful people. It was just a yard.

Frowning, she stomped to the back door, kicked off her stained shoes and stepped inside. There was a great deal of commotion in the office. Her laptop was the first thing that came to mind, and she ran, tripping over a piece of toy racetrack on the way. When her knees smacked the vinyl flooring, she howled in pain.

Annabelle appeared, eyes wide with concern. "Did you fall down?"

Kylee remained on all fours, forehead slumped to the ground while she counted to ten.

"Are you okay, Aunt Kylee?" Henry's voice was comforting, but only a little.

"What are you doing in my room?" she asked in a muffled voice without looking up.

"We're not in *your* room," came Annabelle's reply. "We were in the office."

Kylee sat up. "Doing what?"

Both children fell silent.

She straightened, and Henry pointed at his sister. "She did it."

Annabelle frowned, made a lame effort to punch his shoulder and ran to their bedroom, stepping over the toys in the hall like a prima ballerina.

Kylee gulped. If the little girl was sending herself to her room, it had to be bad. Kylee reached for Henry's hand and braced herself as she climbed to her feet.

When she walked into the office, it took a moment, but a scan around the room showed a wiggly red line on the walls. She looked at Henry. He pointed at the floor. A bright red marker sans cap was lying beside the fold-out couch. Upon closer inspection, Kylee saw that her Hermès handbag was also tattooed with red ink.

"Oh no!" she gasped, and Henry dashed from the room.

Kylee slumped to the floor on her throbbing knees and picked up the purse. She'd spent a large portion of her paycheck on it, rationalizing that it would never go out of style if she took care of it. She took care of all of her belongings. Everything had a place; everything had a purpose. So what was she doing here?

Mia's house was usually semi-cluttered, but since Kylee had been in charge, it looked like a tornado had hit. She couldn't keep up. Everywhere she turned, there was something to clean, and as soon as she started, the twins ran in the opposite direction to take something else apart.

She'd only gotten through half of her emails. The laundry closet in the hall was stacked with piles of clothes, the bathroom hadn't been cleaned, and breakfast and lunch dishes still waited in the kitchen sink. There were also fast-food wrappers on the table although she'd told the children to put them in the trash. She'd been so frazzled after going through a drive-through for lunch with the two chatterboxes in the back seat that she'd brought them home instead of going on a picnic she'd planned.

Kylee's stomach curdled as she examined the purse. She licked a finger and tried to rub the marker off, but it just smeared. She leaned against the couch and shut her eyelids. The sound of books tumbling off the shelf in the room next door reminded her it was reading time; at least that had been Evan's order of activities when she arrived, and she was trying to do familiar things for her sister's children. She looked up at the ceiling, feeling inept and unimportant—the way she'd always felt in this family.

Kylee's eyes misted with frustration. No wonder her parents acted like Mia had accomplished one of the greatest feats on earth giving birth to twins and keeping them alive. It was like playing Whac-A-Mole without the whacker. Kylee had graduated valedictorian from high school, earned a full scholarship to the University of Georgia and could manage a team of a hundred employees, but a pair of four-year-old children was making her look incompetent.

There was another crash, and she decided if the twins made a hole in the wall, she would move to a hotel and hire a nanny. Two of them. Then the doorbell rang, and one of the kids flew down the hall to the front door.

Kylee jumped to her feet, imagining Annabelle racing into the street. Her stomach lurched at the thought of another tragedy, and she dashed into the hall to find her mother standing in the middle of the family room.

Mom swiveled her gaze around the devastation in amazement.

"Mom!" Kylee hurried to throw her arms around her mother.

"Hi, Nanna!" cried Annabelle. "Henry, Nanna's here!" The little girl ran back toward her bedroom.

Mom laughed. "What happened in here? Are you okay?" She patted Kylee's back.

"No. I mean, yes." Kylee sighed and pulled away. She'd forgotten how warm and soft her mother felt when she let down her guard. The familiar smell of her powdery perfume was like a tonic. "The kids are supposed to be in their bedroom. It's reading time."

"Henry, no!" shrieked Annabelle from the other side of the house. "It's my turn." Her voice rattled the windows.

Kylee rolled her eyes. "I mean, it's supposed to be." She shook her head. "But I can't keep them focused on one simple task for more than sixty seconds." Her mother grinned. "I'm serious," Kylee protested. "I timed them."

"Task?"

"They didn't make their beds, and I had to brush their hair and teeth. Henry won't eat any of the Kix cereal I bought them last night, and Annabelle spilled french fries all over Mia's car. And then there's…this." Kylee waved around the house. "I gave them a list of chores to do, but they completely ignored it and made more messes while I was on the phone."

"With who?"

"I'm still helping the office transition to my sub," Kylee explained. She stopped from explaining further how difficult it was to let someone else take over her responsibilities. "There are things only I can do, and I'm having to slowly hand over the reins."

"Oh." Mom sounded abrupt.

"They need to do things right," Kylee insisted. She glanced at her sister's family pictures on the mantel. They weren't all looking at the camera at the same time. "I really need your help."

Her mother smiled at her. "You can do this. I'll do what I can."

"But you can do more than me," Kylee blurted. Her jaw mentally dropped. Had she ever said those words before? Realizing her mother might think she was incapable of managing a household, she corrected herself. "I mean… I just need an extra hand. An assistant."

Mom smiled at her. "It's getting harder for me to get around with the arthritis that comes with this fibromyalgia, but I can help a little. Let me read to the children while you clean up."

Kylee was flooded with guilt and gave her mother another hug, gently this time. To Kylee's surprise, her mother's call for the children to sit on the floor of their bedroom with one book each was heeded like she was the Pied Piper.

As Mom's soft voice droned from the bedroom, Kylee cleaned up the kitchen, family room and hallway. By the time she opened the bifold doors in the hall to evaluate the laundry situation, Mom came out of the bedroom with the twins trotting behind her like obedient colts.

"How was story time?" Kylee asked the children. She felt much calmer and had a spark of new hope for this phase of her life.

"Good," chirped Henry.

"There's a charcuterie board on the counter," she informed them. "Sit with Nanna and eat neatly, then put your plates in the dishwasher."

"Char-tru-tree? That sounds yucky," Annabelle snarled.

"We're not allowed to open the dishwasher," Henry informed her as they trooped by.

Kylee heard her mother chuckle. "It's a little late for snacks, so I'll just give them a cup of milk. What are your plans for dinner?"

Kylee's relaxed mind locked up again. "Stuffed olives and pâté?" she sputtered. "I haven't thought that far ahead. We went to the store before lunch today, and I bought frozen pizzas."

Mom grinned. "Those will do."

Kylee sighed with relief. "I'm so glad you're here. Thanks for the break."

"I don't mind. I know it's a huge undertaking, and we've turned your life upside down."

Kylee nodded, because they had. "Yes, but I can handle it. I just need to get oriented and organized. I'm sorry it took so long for me to get home."

"You're coming along," Mom assured her. She picked up her purse. The fridge door banged shut, and she hurried to the kitchen with Kylee on her heels. Kylee opened her mouth to scold Henry when they found him pouring a cup of milk on the floor.

"Careful now, baby," said his grandmother. Mom put her purse on the counter and slowly crouched down to the floor with a soft moan.

"Oh, Mom," Kylee gasped, remembering how uncomfortable it was for her mother to bend over. "Let me do that!" She helped her mother up, then reached for the cup and jug of milk that Henry would surely have poured all over the floor. "To the table," she ordered him, and he sauntered to his booster seat while she poured two cups of milk. Setting them on the table, she pulled out a chair for her mother. "Here, sit down. I know reading to them is frustrating because they don't listen for very long."

"You don't use the right voices," Henry pointed out. He picked up his cup of milk and sipped.

Annabelle strolled in with her troll doll and announced, "I want milk, too."

"Climb up into your seat like a spider and sip your milk like a princess," Mom told her. To Kylee's shock, the little girl complied. "Don't spill a drop now," her mother warned her. "If you do, you lose."

"And I win," said Henry. He gave his sister a devious smile, his cup clutched in his hand.

Mom looked over her shoulder. "They do have sippy cups, dear, with lids that screw on."

"I saw those," admitted Kylee. "Annabelle said they were for babies."

"Oh, no, they use them all the time." Mom slanted her head at Annabelle, raising one thin eyebrow. "Don't let them fool you. They're tricky."

Annabelle giggled, her eyes glowing with affection for her grandmother.

Kylee observed the exchange, impressed. "You're like the child whisperer," she said in disbelief.

Mom chuckled and slowly climbed to her feet. "I've had plenty of experience, dear. You're a natural born leader, Kylee. You just need to get used to the kids and their personalities. Chaos is a part of parenthood."

"I don't do chaos, Mom." Kylee watched her reach for her purse. "You're not leaving, are you?" Alarm surged in her chest. There was still laundry, the rest of the backyard and dinner.

"Isn't it TV time?" asked Mom.

"Yay!" shouted Henry, overjoyed.

"We tried that yesterday," said Kylee. "They didn't pay attention."

The little boy scowled. "I want to watch *Cicero the Scientist*. Watching fish swim is boring."

"They were spawning," Kylee corrected him. She was certain Mia would have approved of science documentaries. "You might go to Alaska someday. How are you going to know what salmon and grizzlies look like if you don't learn about them?"

The room fell quiet as Henry looked puzzled. Mom pushed her purse strap up over her shoulder and headed for the door. "You *are* right. It is science, but the Cicero cartoon is funny and educational. It keeps their attention."

Kylee resisted the urge to throw herself to the floor and grab her mother's heels to keep her from leaving. She couldn't even choose the right shows for the twins. "I thought you might want to have dinner with us."

Mom reached for the dead bolt. "I have to pick up some things from the pharmacy, then go home and lie down." Her face gave away her fatigue. "I'm supposed to rest two times a day. Doctor's orders. And check my blood pressure. I'm sorry."

"Of course, Mom. It's not a problem." Kylee shrugged as if it was no big deal. "That's why I'm here. I got this."

"I know you do, dear. But don't forget, you can always call Evan if you need something I can't do. He can help you until you head back to New York. Not that I'm looking forward to it."

Kylee stiffened. Evan had already made breakfast on Tuesday. "No. He has a job. Mia left this to me."

"Because she trusted you." Mom blew the twins a kiss

and walked out with no idea how much her words seared Kylee's heart.

Annabelle screeched, "No! Don't go, Nanna!" and jumped up on the table to watch her grandmother walk down the sidewalk through the window. Her foot sideswiped Henry's glass of milk and sent it rolling across the table.

"Annabelle!" Kylee cried. "Henry, get a towel."

"No," he replied. "She did it."

He clambered down from his booster seat and traipsed away while Kylee scooped up a screaming Annabelle, set her firmly on the couch and ran for the mop in the pantry. A piercing pain shot through her lower back, and she stopped to rub it.

She'd assumed she'd have help when she accepted Mia's wish to raise her children, but Mom's health had declined far more than she knew. Her analytical, driven father would have lost his mind handling a pair of littles like this twenty-four-seven if he were still alive. Thank goodness Evan had filled in until she arrived, she admitted. But now it was on Kylee alone. No assistant. No staff. No personal chef or physical trainer. No one cared she had an Hermès bag. Nobody cared that she was the creative director of a Fortune 500 company in New York. Yes, she could hire someone, but a part of her wanted to prove she could do this, too, without help. And do it for her sister.

The television clicked on in the next room. Her choice of nature documentaries the day before hadn't been a hit. She might as well let them watch whatever made them happy.

Kylee staggered back to the kitchen table to clean up the milk spill. The laundry would have to sit. Cleaning the stain on her purse would have to wait. The backyard wasn't going anywhere. She glanced at the clock over the stove and realized it wouldn't be unreasonable to start dinner in a half hour. If the TV could keep the twins entertained for a while, and they ate the frozen pizza she'd bought, she could get them to bedtime without too much trouble.

See? Kylee Spokes could handle two four-year-olds and a little cottage. She didn't need her mother. She didn't need Mia. She certainly didn't need the paramedic. No matter how appealing he was…

Chapter Four

Evan's cell phone rang, cut off, then a few seconds later, rang again. He set his clothes dryer for thirty minutes, then hurried to the kitchen where the lentils in his pressure cooker were cooling. He'd have to eat his dinner lukewarm if he didn't get to them soon.

The phone rang again, and he searched the living room for it, wondering if work needed him early. Finally, on the plaid sofa, camouflaged in the dark blue stripes beside the book he'd finished, was his phone. He flipped it over and checked the caller. It was an unfamiliar number, but something made him answer. "Hello?"

Before he could say anything else, the sounds of a crying child echoed in the background. A calm, businesslike voice asked, "Evan Hollister?"

"Yes. Is that you, Kylee?" The crying continued, a mournful wail like a dog in distress. "What's wrong?" Evan clenched the phone tighter. "Are the kids okay?"

"Yes, they're fine," said Kylee. "Annabelle thinks she's starving to death."

Evan checked the time on the phone, then put it back to his ear. "They usually eat about now—a half hour from now, actually. Can she not eat early?" Was the woman that much of a control freak?

"Oh, it's not that," said Kylee with a rush of impatience. "I made dinner a few minutes ago. She just won't eat it."

"Why not?"

"Apparently, she doesn't like pizza." Kylee sounded shocked. "Neither one of them will eat anything and are crying for macaroni and cheese."

"There should be a box of it somewhere."

"*Your* macaroni and cheese."

Evan understood now. "But they like pizza," he said in confusion.

"Not with leaves on it."

"What?" Evan slapped his forehead.

"It's a meat and veggie pizza. I tried scraping all the toppings off, but she says it still tastes like dirt. Which is hilarious since she licked dirt and soap bubbles all morning."

He chuckled.

"It's not funny," said Kylee in exasperation.

"I know, I just… Yes, they only eat cheese pizza."

"Really? I thought that was a cliché."

"No, it's childhood," laughed Evan.

"Not mine," she said under her breath, but Evan heard her. "I'm sorry to bother you, but I need your macaroni and cheese recipe."

Evan checked his watch again. If Kylee couldn't boil egg noodles, there was no way she'd get his grandmother's macaroni and cheese recipe right. "I'll tell you what. I have to run out to the grocery store and get some cat food for Peppy. I'll grab the fixings for mac and cheese, make it and drop it off." There was a pause on the phone. "I don't mind, and you probably don't have all the ingredients," he added.

"You're probably right. I do have goat cheese, though, and prosciutto."

He groaned.

"Olives?"

"Nope," he said firmly into the phone.

"You said they don't eat junk. I have a charcuterie board."

"Sugar. I said they don't eat a lot of sugar. I didn't say they ate French cuisine."

"Fine," Kylee retorted. "I'll eat the pizza. They can go hungry until you get here."

"I'm sure they'll live." Evan knew he sounded curt. If Kylee would just let him come over in the mornings, he could see what the children needed for the day. After hanging up, he shot James a text that he might be late for his shift, grabbed his keys and headed out.

He'd offered to pick up Peppy's food when Mrs. Lightfoot mentioned she wouldn't have time to swing by the vet for the special formula. After getting the cat food from the nearby clinic, Evan darted into Brook's Grocery up the road from the railroad tracks on the edge of town and grabbed all the ingredients he needed. Back at his apartment, it took another hour to make the mac and cheese. The task made him forget his uniform in the dryer, and when he reached Chip and Mia's house, he was wrinkled and exasperated.

Juggling the hot casserole dish, he rapped on the door he was used to just walking through. It swung open to shouts of joy and Henry hanging from the knob.

Kylee came dashing down the hall in slacks that hit just above her ankles and an untucked short-sleeve shirt. She looked almost charming in bare feet with her hair in a ponytail. Her toes were perfectly pedicured.

He jerked his gaze up, slightly embarrassed, and held out the casserole dish.

"Oh, thank you so much," she exclaimed.

His frustration over her lack of homemaking skills abated. "You're welcome," he said.

She darted to the kitchen with it, and Henry beamed up at him. "Are you going to read to us now?"

"Didn't you read today?"

"She doesn't sound like Wilbur."

Evan grinned, pleased to be recognized for his skills.

"Henry," Kylee called from the kitchen. She hadn't officially invited Evan in, but from the sounds of Annabelle sniffling, she probably needed his help.

Evan shut the door behind him. "Come on, champ," he told Henry. The boy grabbed his hand, and they walked to the kitchen.

Annabelle was lying on the floor beneath the table with tears coursing down her cheeks.

"Annabelle, *please* come out from under the table," Kylee begged.

"No," she moaned.

"Evan brought the food you wanted. Come on." Kylee's tone sharpened. "We have no time for this. It's almost bedtime." She tapped her foot.

Evan crouched down and peeked between a chair and a table leg. "What's the matter, sweetheart?" he murmured.

Annabelle rolled to her knees, crawled out to him and settled in his lap at the table. Evan held her as Henry climbed into his booster seat, and Kylee piled macaroni on his plate.

"I brought you dinner. Aren't you hungry?" Evan whispered in the little girl's ear.

She nodded.

"Then why don't you eat?"

"I want you to come here," she whimpered. "I want Mama…and Daddy." She buried her face against his chest and began to sob.

Evan patted her back. "I'm only a few minutes away. It's going to be okay, sweetie."

Kylee stood at the table with the casserole dish in her hands and her eyes wide with concern. "I didn't mean to make her cry," she said softly.

"You didn't," Evan assured her. "She's sensitive."

"She's hungry," Henry stated.

Evan suspected the twins had been hungry for days. He wiped Annabelle's tears and put a finger under her chin while Kylee carried the casserole dish back to the counter. "It's time to eat dinner, okay? It's your favorite, and you need to put something in your belly if you're going to grow up to be smart and strong."

She nodded at him and climbed up to her seat. He scooted her chair closer to the table. As the children began to chatter back and forth, Evan began picking up the toys scattered all over the family room, surprised Kylee hadn't helped them do it.

She strode in as if hearing his thoughts. "I told them to clean up, but they stopped after a minute," she said in exasperation.

"You have to be specific with them," Evan explained. "And vigilant. They have short attention spans."

"They require a lot more time than I expected," Kylee said. "I can't leave the room or answer texts without something being opened, pulled down or taken apart."

He grinned. "Yes, they need constant attention."

She set down a stuffed toy and collapsed onto the couch. "Annabelle drew all over the office walls and my new purse with red marker."

"Ouch," said Evan. "Just set some boundaries."

"I thought they'd be in school by now."

"Mia had them in a playgroup, and I've been taking them when I can. I suggest you continue."

"I should," agreed Kylee. "Don't they have preschool here?"

"Yes, but it's a lottery system to get into pre-K. Your mother and I weren't sure that it was best for them because Mia wasn't, and it was too late to apply."

"I've already sent an application to the best school in Manhattan so they should be able to get some childcare and instruction before next school year," she said.

Evan frowned. "Mia never wanted them in a preschool when they could make ends meet on Chip's income and she could teach them."

"What about rules? You know, boundaries?" Kylee raised her brows at him.

"I'm all for rules in the right context," agreed Evan. Kylee obviously knew how to organize an army; she just didn't understand her audience here. Even he had needed time to get used to Chip and Mia being gone and how to handle the twins. Maybe Kylee just needed time, too. But she was a fish out of water in Lagrasse, and she didn't seem interested in learning how to fit in. "I'm happy to make dinner a couple times a week if that would help," he offered.

Her eyes darted toward the now-contented children. "I... I guess that's a good idea since they're used to seeing you." Then she added, "Maybe you could read to them, too."

A flicker of hope lit Evan's heart. "No problem. It'd give you a break." Maybe if Kylee let him help more, she'd see he was the better option to be the twins' guardian. He leaned forward on his knees. "Would you like to work out a schedule?" he suggested. "I'll come over and read to them and start dinner." He watched her hesitate. "It'd give you time alone to run errands and do things you need to do."

She seemed to relax. "I guess a few hours to myself is a good idea. I could check in at work, too."

"I'm open to it," Evan pressed. "I could even help you at church."

Her attention flitted to the children at the table again. "That's not something I'm worried about right now."

Evan shouldn't have been surprised when she jumped up to retrieve her phone. He wondered if he should mention the upcoming annual Nativity at Good Shepherd Church, but then she dropped back beside him on the couch in a cloud of flowery smelling shampoo that made him forget about the twins.

Exotic. Mysterious. *Gardenia?* Somehow it complemented her olive complexion and dark eyes and hair. Her shoulder brushed his, and a sudden current radiated from his chest down to the palms of his hands. *What on earth?* Kylee? The bossy-pants boardroom president? She was so… frustrating. Stubborn. Difficult. Evan cleared his throat and reached for his phone to pull up his calendar.

Kylee's hickory-brown eyes met his. "What are your shifts like on Tuesdays and Thursdays?"

Evan pulled his attention away from her and went back to his phone to stop examining her oval face. Sharp cheekbones. Soft chin. "I have to be in by 8:00 p.m. most of the time," he replied. "I can come at four in the afternoon and stay until seven," he offered.

She hesitated, and somehow he knew she was calculating her hours as if she had to clock in and out to prove herself.

"You can check in on your mom or whatever," he added.

"And you'll cook on those days if I don't?" she clarified.

Evan felt some amusement bubble up, but he fought back a chuckle. "Sure. I'll make dinner." He didn't miss her subtle exhale of relief.

"I suppose that would give you time to spend with them like you used to."

Evan couldn't help but wonder what Kylee would do on the days he didn't come over. "What about weekends?"

She thought for a minute, then turned to him. "I'll reserve some books online at the library or take them to Murphy's Bookstore. They can browse. My mom will help on the weekends if she's up to it."

Browse? The twins would pull books off the shelves like toys. He bit the inside of his cheek to keep from smiling. Regardless, he would do the storytelling. Sounded like a good plan. "Deal. The playgroup usually meets on Tuesdays, so you'd be able to see some other mothers," he suggested, although she didn't seem interested in making friends.

"Perfect." Kylee turned off her phone and set it down.

"And maybe you can reconsider attending church? We have an annual Nativity that the twins won't want to miss." Evan held his breath. The event was important to him, to the children.

"I'll think about it."

"The Nativity was something Chip and Mia participated in every year with the kids."

Kylee didn't seem swayed.

Henry wandered in, picked up a dinosaur and held it out. "Can you play with me now, Evan?"

"Evan has to get to work," said Kylee somewhat reluctantly.

He pulled out his phone and saw that he was indeed late for his shift. "I have to go, buddy." He pointed at Kylee. "I bet Aunt Kylee is an awesome Tyrannosaurus rex." He hurried for the door to avoid seeing the reaction on her face. "See you later, Annabelle!" he called.

"Bye, Evan! I'm going to be a dinosaur, too," she roared.

Evan couldn't stop grinning the entire way to the firehouse. Poor Kylee. She had no idea what playing dinosaurs meant. He couldn't imagine her on her hands and knees chasing the kids through the house. He hoped she had good reflexes because pillows would be flying in every direction. Then again, a few hours of being attacked by dinosaurs just might send her running back to New York for good.

Chapter Five

The next Tuesday, Kylee was dressed before the dinosaurs arose, just minutes after a loud school bus rumbled down the street. The weekend hadn't felt like a weekend. The bookstore outing had been a disaster.

She grabbed a canister of quick-cooking grits from the pantry. They only took a minute and a half in the microwave, and neither of the twins noticed they weren't from scratch. She felt like she'd just won a round in the boardroom, but there was no time to celebrate because there were beds to make and laundry to begin. She'd never before dealt with mounds of laundry like the children made, but since today was their playgroup at the park, she crammed the washer full to get it all done at once. She assumed double duty meant double the detergent, so she was generous with that, too.

"Shoes on!" she called out like a drill sergeant, checking her smartwatch. There were no sounds coming from the twins' bedroom, so she repeated herself and added, "I'm leaving in five, four, three…" She faded off as Annabelle cried out.

Turning the dial to start the washing machine, Kylee slammed the laundry closet doors in the hall shut and hurried to the kitchen for her ink-stained purse. There were still dirty dishes in the sink, but they would have to wait.

Annabelle and Henry were strangely obedient. Their shoes were untied, their shirts untucked, and their hair looked like scarecrows', but she didn't have to drag them out to the minivan this time.

They drove to the center of town where a large park was surrounded by historical buildings that housed gift and antique stores along with a clothing consignment shop. Other small food businesses nearby released tempting aromas into the air, and Kylee's mouth watered as she led the kids to a playground beside a Victorian-inspired water fountain. Her heart tugged with nostalgia. She'd hung out with study groups on pleasant days here after school. There'd been laughter. Companionship. Good times.

"Ava!" shouted Annabelle, and she ripped away from Kylee's hand before she could stop her.

A group of people had congregated at a bench, and a familiar face turned. It only took seconds for Kylee to thumb through the roster in her mind: Pamela Sturgess. She gave her old classmate a meek smile, hoping she remembered her. They'd been in the same class during elementary school and taken a few subjects together in high school.

The pear-shaped woman with shoulder-length hair put a hand on her hip, her large round eyes crinkling at the corners. "Why, if it isn't Kylee Spokes! Valedictorian and most successful Lagrasse Tiger of her class."

Kylee felt herself redden, but her cheeks ached when she smiled wide. "Hi, Pamela. It's been a long time." She looked around as Annabelle and Henry scurried around like chickens with their flock of friends.

"I'm so sorry about Mia," said Pamela. "We miss her. I heard you were coming back to town to take care of the twins. Your mother told my mother at the Rotary."

"I'm sure she did," chuckled Kylee.

Pamela gave her a once-over. "How have you kept in shape? You look wonderful."

One of the other women with a baby on her hip joined them with a giggle. "You don't gain weight walking the streets of New York, I bet," she teased. "Hi, I'm Ali Underwood." She held out a hand for Kylee to shake. "My husband and I go to Good Shepherd Church with your mom and Evan. He said you might be joining us here today."

"Hi." Kylee smiled, unable to resist the warmhearted welcome.

"And this is my cousin, Tam," continued Ali. "She owns The Gracious Earth herb shop down the street."

A cheerful, fair brunette gave Kylee a grin. "I heard all about you at the bakery when Evan came in. Welcome back to Lagrasse."

There was no insincerity in this group. No coworker to outmaneuver. No supervisor to impress. It was a welcome relief. "I'm happy to be here. I sure needed a break because these kids have a lot of energy."

"Oh, they sure do," laughed Pamela, "and you get a double dose."

A woman the others called Gretchen nodded. "Ava is my daughter. My oldest, Ella, is in school." She pointed at Annabelle's companion. "Ava and Annabelle have known each other since they were babies."

Kylee smiled. "That explains all the 'Ava says' remarks I've been hearing."

Gretchen and Pamela laughed.

Pamela brushed a hand across her heart. "I'm Pamela Maynard now." She nodded toward a short slide painted bright yellow. Three boys were chasing each other around it, including Henry. "The rascal in the green turtle shirt is Tyler. He's five. We're holding him back a year."

"From kindergarten?" Kylee said in surprise.

Pamela motioned for the others to join her on the bench. "He isn't quite ready, in my opinion, and he is my baby," she admitted. "He's already enjoying sports, and it doesn't hurt to have him be the oldest in his grade. He'll be bigger in the long run."

"You can do that?" Kylee raised her brows.

Pamela shrugged.

How clever, thought Kylee, strangely appreciating the maneuvering. She looked up into the sprawling branches of an ancient tree, recalling that it had been here long before she left, and sat down surprised at how comfortable the iron bench felt in the sunshine. "It smells wonderful out here. Where's that coming from?"

"The Last Re-Torte, no doubt." Gretchen pointed at a silver-coiffed woman in a white untucked linen shirt and blue jeans playing with Ava and Annabelle. "That's my mom, Donna. She owns the bakery but helps with Ava when she's not at preschool."

"I've been wondering why the twins weren't in preschool," said Kylee. "Evan said there was a lottery system and that he didn't apply."

Gretchen nodded. "Yes, but there are other programs at some of the churches, and we have a playgroup."

Kylee nodded, but she wouldn't be staying in town long enough to enroll the children anywhere locally. "I'm sure the twins will be ready socially," she said.

Pamela waved her off. "Oh, don't worry. They'll adapt even if they're a few steps behind. I'm on my fourth."

"Fourth?" repeated Kylee, impressed.

Pamela grinned just as Tyler ran up and dropped a rock in her open palm. "Yes, three in my twenties and then this wonderful surprise."

Tyler darted a suspicious look at Kylee, which made her regret wearing designer jeans and a white cashmere hoodie.

"You're amazing," said Kylee.

"She is," interjected Tam. "I only have one in sixth grade, and I'm about to lose my mind."

"Oh, you're doing fine," laughed her cousin, Ali. She smiled at her little girl. "I have a nine-year-old son in school, and this is Alice."

Kylee smiled at the beautiful baby, and a strange longing suddenly curled around her heart.

"Are you married?" asked Pamela. Her steady stare hinted that she was trying not to look down at Kylee's ring finger. "I understand you work in corporate."

Kylee shook her head. "No. I mean yes. I work for Digital Rock as Creative Director. I lead teams that help companies get exposure, build their brands and increase online activity so they can grow. Right now I'm on leave, but I call in about three times a week, and there's a group chat for emergencies."

"Will you go back?"

"Yes, just before Christmas."

"Hmm," sang Pamela. "Maybe you'll change your mind and stay in town."

Kylee chuckled. "No, I'm afraid not. I enjoy the city too much. Always did."

"What about Atlanta?" piped up Gretchen.

"Oh, I… Well," Kylee faltered. "It's not New York."

"I suppose not," said Pamela with a faint smile. "But we sure could use someone of your management experience on the PTA board. We have a lot of committees."

Ava let out a high-pitched screech from the top of the slide that made Kylee's hair stand on end, and just before she launched herself from the bench to rescue her, the women around her broke into laughter.

"Did you actually jump?" teased Pamela.

"I guess I did," Kylee chuckled. "Annabelle and Henry keep me on my toes."

"Oh, just wait until they're tweens," warned Pamela.

They sat back to watch the children while peppering Kylee with questions about her work, then explained what was expected when the twins started kindergarten.

Kylee smiled and nodded, but her chest began to squeeze tighter and tighter. Could Annabelle write her name? Did Henry know how to read? She hadn't considered that besides being cook, housekeeper and chauffeur, she had to teach another human being the alphabet and how to count to one hundred. *I have to get back to New York. They've got to get into a preschool.*

Her smile grew stiffer, but she managed to bluff her way through conversation, relieved when it turned to old times and memories—parties at the lake, prom and who'd married whom or joined the armed forces. Those things were comfortable. There were no more mentions of Mia— the athlete, the volunteer of the month, the homecoming queen—but Tam did invite Kylee to church and the annual Christmas Nativity.

It'd been a while since she'd set foot in the Good Shepherd Church. Any church. Sure, she'd been in one for the funeral, but she hadn't made time for a spiritual life in New York. She'd told herself that God expected her to work hard to make something of herself, so she worked long hours all week and tried to catch up on her sleep on Sunday mornings instead. But that'd been an excuse, she realized. She'd made it all about herself and put God second. It was time to pivot. Between losing Mia and taking on the twins, it was time to turn back to the one source of strength who had never let her down.

Evan rose groggily from his cot and realized his shift was over. He immediately checked his watch. It was just before lunch. The twins should be with their playgroup right now. He wondered if Kylee had listened to his advice and decided to stroll down to the park. If the twins were there and restless, they might enjoy a walk back to the firehouse. He could offer Kylee an early break rather than show up in the late afternoon. He climbed off the cot to wash up, wondering how Kylee would interact with the other mothers.

Minutes later, he was strolling down Main Street. Christmas decorations would take center stage soon, but rather than cheer him up, it weighed on him. Once the red ribbons and bows and holiday greenery went up after Thanksgiving, everyone would start talking about the upcoming holiday and, of course, the children's Nativity.

There was no getting out of the annual Nativity with the determined widow Sister Lovell, as she liked to be called, dogging him about it. And of course, the twins were looking forward to playing sheep as their grandmother had lately promised when it was mentioned. Mia and Chip were usually Mary and Joseph. His chest squeezed. What an awful Christmas it would be, when there was nothing to be joyful about this year. Not for him. Not after he'd lost his best friends.

Shoulders drooping, Evan trudged on to the park. The lively playground was full of children of all ages running here and there, enjoying the day. He checked his watch. The playgroup would have ended a few minutes ago. He surveyed the swarm of youngsters.

"Hi, Evan," called Ali. The local beekeeper grinned at him. "Looking for the twins?"

"Yes. I thought I'd check on them before I went home."

"You're just off work?"

He nodded at her question.

"I thought I'd have lunch here with Alice." She slanted her head at a little one picking through the grass at her feet, then pointed toward a grove of trees. "Annabelle is up in the General's oak tree. They're trying to get her down."

"What?" Evan wasn't sure if he should be surprised or concerned, but he gave Ali a fleeting wave and jogged toward the park benches. Sure enough, a circle of parents stood beneath the tallest oak looking up.

Straddling a high limb with her arms hugging a huge branch, Annabelle had a mischievous grin on her face.

"Annabelle!" he called as he raced to the tree. Where was Kylee?

"I was just on my way to the car," said Pamela Maynard. "And there she was waving at everyone."

"Hi, Evan!" called Annabelle. "Look at me!"

"Get down here right now. You know that's not safe."

"No," said Annabelle.

"Where's your moth—" Evan caught himself. "Where's Kylee?" Annabelle did not have a mother. Because of him.

"She went that way." Annabelle pointed across the street, and Evan frowned as storm clouds brewed in his chest.

"How did you even get up there?" he demanded, seeing the answer before the words left his mouth. She had climbed up the back of the bench no doubt, reached the lowest branch, swung herself up and then climbed. "Please come down before you hurt yourself."

"I don't want to," she complained.

"If you fall, you'll have to go to the hospital," warned Evan. "You might break your arm."

That seemed to do the trick, but with a stab of guilt Evan realized that the word *hospital* had dark connotations for her. It was where her parents had been taken, where she'd been seated in a private waiting room before the pastor came in. Where they heard the bad news about their parents. "Climb down so you can stay safe," he said.

She scowled. "I can't. I'm stuck."

Evan hopped up onto the bench beneath her. He braced himself and held out his arms. "I'm right here. Jump." He spotted her as she dropped down and hung from the branch like a long-armed gibbon. Wrapping his arms around her, he eased her to the ground just as Kylee appeared, out of breath and carrying Henry against her hip like a rag doll.

"Oh, good," she panted. "You got her down."

"Why did you let her get up there? Don't you know she could have fallen?"

Kylee stared, speechless for a few seconds. "I left her on the bench. Henry disappeared, and I had to go look for him. I didn't know she could climb trees!"

"She's a child. She can climb anything," retorted Evan. His heart galloped in his chest, and he tried to calm the adrenaline that had erupted upon seeing Annabelle up in the tree. He frowned, remembering Kylee had abandoned her to go across the street. "Where'd you let Henry go?"

"I was trying to stop Annabelle from throwing wood chips, and he decided to go get himself a cupcake. I put her on the bench and ran down there." Kylee pointed in the direction of the bakery.

"The Last Re-Torte?"

"Yes, that's it. Charming little place. I almost bought

one myself." Kylee smiled and seemed to forget that either of the children could have been seriously injured.

"Are you serious? Cupcakes? Annabelle might have fallen, and Henry could have been hit by a car."

"There's only one of me," said Kylee in exasperation. "Do you think you could have done better?" Her words were soaked with unspoken accusation.

No, he couldn't have done better. First aid skills would not have stopped the twins from running in two different directions. He couldn't control everything—or save everyone. He'd proven that.

"Maybe playgroup isn't a good idea," he said.

To his surprise, Kylee said, "Playgroup is a great idea." She was unaware that the twins were watching their back-and-forth like it was a volleyball game. "They played with their friends, and their friends stayed by their parents until the last few minutes."

"Maybe you should leave before the rest of the group does," Evan grunted.

Kylee crossed her arms over her chest. "I'm sorry my parenting skills aren't on par with your expectations. I told you my only experience was with interns. Maybe if there were penalties for their behavior, they would follow orders."

"What are you going to do? Fine them?" Evan quipped. "Demote them?"

"Funny," snapped Kylee. "If Mia had—"

"You have no idea how Mia raised her children," he said in a low tone. "You weren't around, were you?"

"Well, I'm here now." Kylee's retort sounded confident and challenging, as lightning flashed in her eyes.

"I'm here to help, Kylee."

"Why don't you take them both home for lunch then, and I'll be right behind you?"

"Fine," said Evan. "I'm sure they would rather read anyway."

"Enjoy your time with them. I'm going to get a cupcake."

His time with them. If her plans to leave by Christmas were set, his time with them was running short. He looked down at Henry, who was listening to everything with wide eyes. "It's okay, champ," Evan assured him.

"Are you angry at Aunt Kylee?" asked Henry with concern.

"No, we're not mad. We're just having a grown-up discussion."

He heard Kylee sigh, then she walked away, heading to the bakery, he guessed.

"Where are you going, Aunt Kylee?" Annabelle screeched.

Kylee must have been out of hearing range, because she didn't respond.

Henry stepped closer to Evan. Annabelle rested her chin on Evan's shoulder and watched her aunt leave. "Where's Aunt Kylee going?" Annabelle whimpered again, then buried her face in Evan's neck. Evan knew the little girl's anxiety appeared whenever anyone left her. Not to mention, he'd lashed out at Kylee in his panic. It was rude and wrong. He'd upset them, and, he realized, he needed them—both.

Chapter Six

Evan slumped over the table in the firehouse kitchen with his hands clasped in his lap. The book he'd borrowed from Shawna about an apocalyptic natural disaster hadn't been enough to distract him. A basketball game echoed from the TV in the day room, but all he could think about was his problems. That included Kylee.

Not only did she plan to take the children away, but she couldn't control them. He should have known by the way they ran all over her at home that taking them out in public would be a disaster. She drove through the take-out windows when they went out to eat because a trip into a restaurant with them would be a circus. He sighed.

James walked into the kitchen with a glass and rinsed it at the sink. "Are you okay, man?"

Evan shook his head and remained mute.

James pulled out a chair beside him. "Still worried about the kids?"

"More than ever." Evan crumpled a straw wrapper, then smoothed it out and wrapped it around his finger.

"What'd she do now?"

"It's what she didn't do. Annabelle climbed up in the General's Tree and got stuck yesterday, while Henry crossed the square and made it to the bakery on his own."

"Oh wow," said James in concern. "Are they okay?"

Evan grunted. "It takes a village, you know. People at the park kept an eye on Annabelle while Kylee ran to find Henry."

"They didn't get hurt?"

"No." Evan folded his arms. "But imagine what might have happened."

"Worst-case scenarios," said James. "I raised three kids. You can't watch them every second."

"I do," Evan insisted. "I don't let them out of my sight unless they're with Mrs. Spokes or—well, it's Kylee now—because I don't have a choice."

"When does she take over custody?"

"It's supposed to be official by the end of the year." Storm clouds gathered in his chest again. "Can you imagine if today happened in New York? It's a big city. They have no business going there."

"I'm sure they'll be fine. I was born in Brooklyn, you know. There are nice parks. Good schools. Lots of culture. If she can do that for them, why not?"

"Because it's not…safe," argued Evan.

James raised his salt-and-pepper-colored eyebrows. "There are good people and bad people everywhere, Evan. The location doesn't matter. Sure, Lagrasse is smaller, and there's a lack of good Philly cheesesteaks, but I don't think it's better. There are positives and negatives for different places."

Evan snorted. "Sometimes it seems like she only cares about her career." At least that was how it came off to him. "She left town and never looked back."

"Eh," said James, shrugging it off. "Maybe she loves New York because she loves the energy and what she does.

That'd make anyone happy. And they aren't exactly known for having big kitchens in most New York apartments."

Kylee clearly loved her job. She had no need to know how to cook living in New York with her salary. And the size of Mia and Chip's house did seem to overwhelm her when the twins pulled all of the toys out.

James got to his feet and rested a hand on Evan's shoulder. "The twins are going to be fine. They have two extra angels watching over them, and you and Kylee make four. And remember, the position for lieutenant is still available."

"I'm working on my résumé, but I've been distracted."

"You're going to have to work together until you have to let them go." James walked off.

Evan knew his boss was right, and that he needed to accept it: Kylee was going to take the twins back to New York with her. What would Mia and Chip want him to do until then? At the very least, they'd want him to help and encourage Kylee so the twins would be happy and safe in their new home. But that was not enough. He needed to have an attitude of faith until God showed him why he couldn't raise them himself.

Lights flashed, and the firehouse alarm bells rattled in a deafening clatter. Evan clutched his heart in surprise before stumbling to his feet. At the moment, he had a responsibility to be there for someone else. There was even the lieutenant's job application to finish.

It was time to focus on what he'd been trained to do.

Evan sauntered out to his SUV on Thursday, feeling the bite of a brisk breeze in the sunshine. Mr. and Mrs. Lightfoot were in the front yard with boxes of Christmas decorations. He waved to them as he backed out of the driveway.

Less than ten minutes later, he pulled along the curb of

Chip's house, noting that the yard needed to be raked. Telling himself yard work was not an excuse to spend more time here, he grabbed some washable finger paints he'd picked up at the discount store and headed for the door. He knocked and turned the knob, but it was locked. That was good. It meant the twins hadn't escaped, but it was strangely quiet. He tapped again and hearing nothing, walked around to the back in concern.

The children's voices became audible as he rounded the corner. A squeal from a hammock made him grin. Annabelle and Henry were pushing a hammock with all their might, and it swung back and forth while Kylee clutched the edges of it with her hands. She threw her head back and laughed as gold-and-rust-colored leaves fluttered down from the trees overhead. Her light olive skin and dark eyes glowed in the sunshine. Annabelle collapsed to the ground, laughing at her aunt's pleadings for mercy. Henry continued to give it all he had.

Kylee spotted Evan on the upswing. "Help me!" she cried in between laughter and shrieks.

He walked over, and Henry looked up at him. "I'm trying to swing her to the sky," he explained.

"That's where Mommy and Daddy are," said Annabelle, rising to her feet. She wrapped her arms around one of Evan's legs. "Will you help us?"

"Why do you want to swing Aunt Kylee to heaven?" he teased. "Don't you need her down here?"

"No," said Annabelle, but Henry stopped abruptly as if considering it. "What's that?" Annabelle asked, pointing at the colored bottles under his arm.

"It's paint."

"I like to paint."

"I know you do."

Kylee swung a leg over the hammock to stop herself. Her hair was messy, and he almost reached out to smooth it but caught himself. "You brought paint?" she asked. Her brown eyes widened. "Have you lost your mind?"

He smiled at her. "I thought it'd be a good outdoor activity since it's not too cold today."

"Your circus," she relented, but her tone suggested she was impressed. She climbed out of the hammock and stood up. "It's reading time, and I have some things I need to do," she told the children.

"I want to paint," pouted Annabelle.

"Don't you want to find out what happens to Wilbur?" Evan prodded. "Do you think Charlotte will be able to save him with her spiderwebs?"

"She's a very good friend," said Henry.

"She's *some pig*," cackled Annabelle.

"That's Wilbur!" cried Henry.

"Okay," said Kylee, calling the children to order. "Let's go."

They headed for the back door still chattering as Kylee and Evan followed close behind.

"I'm sorry about the other day," he began quietly. "The whole situation... I overreached."

She was silent for a step, then replied, "I'm sorry, too. I was taking it all in—the parents, the playground—and in a split second the kids were gone in two different directions. I need to come up with a better plan." She scrunched her forehead. "Like microchips."

"Let the other mothers help you," Evan encouraged her. "You'd be surprised how many people are willing to lend a hand."

"I'll do that. Or buy leashes," she joked. "How do you do it?"

"I tell them they're buddies and can't go anywhere without the other, or I assign them to a friend. Then I walk in circles around the playground like a sheepdog."

Kylee chuckled. "I guess sitting and chatting on the benches is out until they get a little older."

"It's a balancing act," Evan admitted.

"They didn't eat their lunch, so they'll be hungry for dinner," she informed him as they walked into the house. "And I couldn't get some grits out of a bowl. They're like cement."

He chuckled. "Yes, you have to rinse any dishes with grits right away. What'd they have for lunch? Peanut butter and jelly?"

She gave a helpless shrug. "I gave that up before I was twelve. I made them prosciutto and cheese sandwiches, but with mayo like Mia liked."

Evan bit down on his tongue, and instead of laughing, said, "They aren't big on lunch meat."

"Or meat in general."

He nodded. She was catching on. Maybe there was hope for her yet.

"I don't have errands to run today, so I'm going to work on Mia's room. Mom asked me to get it cleaned out."

"Do you need help?"

"No, I..." Kylee paused. "I'll do it myself."

He understood. "I guess it needs to be done before you go."

"Yes, I haven't decided whether to rent or sell for now but..." She looked straight ahead at the back door. "I went through my dad's things for them after he passed. Mia couldn't bear it." She gave Evan a sideways glance. "It never occurred to me we wouldn't all live to ripe old ages, you know?"

He nodded, suddenly filled with sympathy for the woman beside him, who had now lost almost all of the family she had. "You're in good health. I'm sure you'll probably see a hundred."

Kylee groaned. "I don't know about that. Getting close to forty is frightening enough."

He chuckled. He was thirty-four, but he understood. They both reached for the back door handle at the same time, fingers fumbling, and in a flash Evan noticed her all at once—fruity, floral, soft and warm. She was different than her sister; not as fair, and more poised and mysterious somehow. The pit of Evan's stomach dropped as if he'd just crested the top of a roller coaster. He braced himself in surprise as a flood of attraction washed over him. He dropped his hand, and she glanced at him strangely and let herself in.

As he followed, he made the conscious choice to avert his eyes from the gentle slope of her shoulders, ignoring how her jeans accentuated her legs. He gave her a meek nod when he passed her as she let herself into her sister and brother-in-law's room.

She had memories to tackle, and he had a pair of twins to wrangle.

A jewelry box stood on Mia's dresser like an urn, the lamps on the bedside tables like gravestones. The silent room was coated with a light layer of dust. Mom had cleaned it at some point, then sealed it up like a tomb. Even the shades were drawn.

The stillness made the beat of her heart audible, and Kylee walked to the bed and sat on the corner to calm it. She liked being around Evan. He made her slow down. See. Listen. Think. In ways she'd always wished she could. Clasping his warm hand as they both reached for the back door had jolted her senses and sent her heart racing. It was unnerving.

She exhaled. If she closed her eyes and concentrated on scents beyond lavender-washed linens and polished wood floors, she could smell Mia. Smiles and sunshine. Laughter and light.

Kylee's chest heaved, and she took a small gasp, realizing she'd held her breath.

A Bible on the bedside table testified to Mia's faith and devotion to the Shepherd. Her heart throbbed. Mia had been a good girl. A good woman. A good mother. Kylee's chest pinched with guilt. Mia had not been a bad sister, she'd just been... Tears welled in Kylee's eyes, spilling over and falling down her cheeks. *Perfect.* Yes, they'd had their squabbles, but mostly over Mia's refusal to follow orders. She'd definitely had a mind of her own, too.

Kylee chuckled, but her smile faded. Mia had married the love of her life, created a beautiful home and brought the twins into the world without apologies for the changes in her dreams, focus and even her body. She hadn't needed a career to shine.

What I do is important, thought Kylee, but Mia had done an important thing, too. The road to success was not a single-lane highway. There were exits, and even shoulders on the road. In their own ways, both sisters had made the world a better place. Kylee felt herself slump. All these years she'd wanted to be the accomplished one because she'd lacked her sister's charm, but Mia had lived her life successfully, too. Just differently. And with no hint of competition.

Kylee scanned the photos littered across the dresser. Stuck in one corner was a small studio portrait of Mia and Kylee at ages two and seven. In it, Kylee was missing a tooth. They both wore Easter dresses and were holding hands.

She took in a deep breath. Mia had kept a picture of them in her room? Emotion leaped into her throat, and she rubbed her eyes and temples. When she looked again, the room seemed a little brighter, the afternoon sunshine striking the covered windows. Kylee told herself her eyes had adjusted, that was all.

Choosing to find peace in the silence over the opposing feelings tumbling through her veins, she climbed to her feet and started with the dresser, pulling all of the drawers open. Her mind automatically started outlining categories for the piles she would create on the floor.

Giggles cascaded through the door. *Templeton has done something funny*, she thought. Despite all of the sneaky rat's behavior in the book, he was, in the end, truly a friend.

With a faint sigh, she reached for the T-shirts first, learning more about who her sister had been. The first one she pulled out was an old Backstreet Boys concert shirt that Mia had swiped from Kylee's closet and never given back. She smiled faintly and folded it neatly to save for herself. Next, she shook open a white-and-black jersey that made a laugh gurgle in her throat. *Sisters Before Misters*. It was obviously an old favorite but ironic because Mia had loved Chip with all her heart. Her life proved it.

Kylee wondered if it'd all been worth it, if having a family had made her sister proud and fulfilled her. Could such a thing really be? No power, no privilege, no paycheck. She chewed her lip. Maybe her sister hadn't been the attention seeker she'd always accused her of being. Maybe, just maybe, Kylee had been wrong.

Chapter Seven

Evan was layering his favorite spaghetti casserole that the twins ate like it was going out of style when he noticed Kylee came out of Mia's bedroom. There were dark pink splotches under her eyes. She'd been quiet, making only the occasional rustle for the past couple of hours. The children seemed to have forgotten she was there—it was usual for Kylee to go out when he came into the house. A rerun of *Cicero the Scientist* was playing on the TV as he sprinkled cheese across the top of the pasta.

When Kylee walked into the kitchen, she cleared her throat like she had a speech to make but didn't say anything. Evan moved as she skirted around him to reach for a water glass, and her hip grazed his. He felt a slow burn creep to his chest. She seemed in no mood to chat, much less argue, but having her around and not issuing directions was disconcerting.

She wandered into the living room, and when he looked in her direction on his way to the oven, he saw she'd seated herself between the twins. Henry unconsciously leaned his head against her arm while she studied Annabelle with a look of sadness. Then affection flickered across her face.

The tender expression made the warmth in Evan's chest spin like a kaleidoscope, and he had to walk away when he saw her crook her neck and plant a kiss on the top of the little girl's head. Was he doing the right thing, discussing the custody of the twins with other people and not informing her of his wishes?

Smells of garlic, tomato, basil and oregano soon filled the house, and when dinner was ready, Kylee set the table and seated the twins. After they'd eaten, Kylee said, "That was wonderful. You sit, and I'll clean up."

Evan took her up on the offer. After she'd cleared the table and put the dishes into the dishwasher, he was surprised when she joined him and the twins in their room.

"Let's play a family game," Annabelle suggested, pulling out a board game.

"Yes," agreed Henry. He looked to the door where Kylee stood watching. "Play with us, Aunt Kylee."

She looked at her phone. "I think it's time for Evan to go to work now. You don't want him to be late."

"I have a couple extra hours," he admitted, checking his watch. "They pushed my shift back tonight."

Kylee dropped down beside him on the floor and sat cross-legged. The game proved to be hysterical fun, as the four of them tried to flip rings onto a plastic whale's spout. Kylee giggled as hard as Annabelle.

Evan loved seeing the twins so happy and carefree. For a moment, the pain and anxiety of their current situation was forgotten in the security of knowing they were loved. Kylee's detailed guidance came in handy as she helped them understand a little geometry, and he marveled at her intelligence and cool head. Then to his astonishment, Henry beat them all and was congratulated with cheers, except from Annabelle, who grunted and frowned.

Evan chided her. "It's a game for fun," he reminded her. "It's not important. You need to be a good sport, and that means being happy for your brother because he won. Only Henry's happiness is important right now."

"But what about mine?" she complained.

"How about a hug and song, and then I'll tuck you into bed before I go?" Evan suggested to distract her.

Kylee raised her brows dramatically and looked at Annabelle. "That means I'm going to tuck in Henry!" she exclaimed with an exaggerated dinosaur growl.

Henry gave a pretend moan and dashed for the bathroom to brush his teeth, and Kylee laughed and chased him out.

By the time the twins were in bed, Evan realized it'd gone so smoothly he still had time before he needed to leave for work. He strolled into the kitchen and saw that it was spotless.

Kylee came in on his heels, bumping into him. "Sorry," she chuckled.

He studied her. "You certainly know how to make a kitchen shine."

She put a hand on her hip. "I do know how to clean," she said, as if mildly offended. "It's just difficult when you have children underfoot."

"You even wiped down the cabinets."

She seemed to blush as she reached into the fridge and pulled out a container of chocolate pudding. "Look what I made for tonight." She held it up. "Want some?"

Evan opened his mouth to say that he should probably go, but instead he said, "I'd love to."

She grabbed two spoons out of a drawer before he could reach for any other dishes, so he followed her to the couch. When she sat down, he reached for the remote, then stopped himself.

"Did you want to watch more Cicero?" he joked, and she laughed with a spoon full of pudding in her mouth. He flipped through the channels and found a charming holiday romance flick that looked rather interesting. He glanced at her. "How do you feel about these movies?"

"Love them," she replied. "I think they're sweet and a fun escape."

Evan was too embarrassed to admit he agreed, although he only watched Christmas romances with his mom, and sometimes with Mia and Chip when Mia insisted. The films were romantic, and he loved the holiday spirit they evoked.

He smiled as Kylee passed him the pudding bowl, and they sat side by side watching the story unfold, her snorting on occasion and him feeling his cheeks warm at every whisper of romantic attraction. It didn't take long to catch up on the storyline, and they enjoyed the next hour as a widowed baker and a businessman from the big city fell in love. He set the bowl on the table after scraping it clean when she offered him the last bite. The room suddenly felt chilly as the movie went to commercial.

"Do you want me to turn on the fire?" he asked, and when she nodded, he got up and flicked the dial on the fireplace, igniting electric flames that made the faux logs glow. He settled back on the couch, wondering if he should turn on another lamp. The room was dim from nightfall. The fake flames danced with one another as the house fell quiet, the only exception the low hum of the television he'd turned down. Another movie began in the background; it looked like it was set in Alaska.

Evan exhaled and leaned back on the couch beside Kylee again, keeping an obvious distance between them. The peacefulness seemed to make her forget her to-do list and responsibilities for the time being. She was staring at the flames, her mood seemingly back to what it was when she exited her sister's room. He studied the glow of the fire reflected in her eyes. "You don't sit still often, do you?" he said in a quiet voice.

Her eyes shifted to him for a brief moment. "Not lately." She cleared her throat. "I've never been one to do that. It makes me feel like I'm falling behind or missing something important."

He smiled and followed her gaze to the fireplace. "Important things rarely disappear. Unless they're urgent, there's always an opportunity. I think the end of the year can make us feel rushed with the holidays and all, but there's always time… I mean, until there's not." He couldn't help but think of Mia and Chip. They'd been rushing home after a date night so Mrs. Spokes could get home after babysitting.

"That's why I'm so schedule-oriented," Kylee admitted. "A deadline is always a possible failure to me, and I… Well, I can't bear it—failure, I mean."

"You are the last person I would ever call a failure," said Evan in amazement.

After a moment's silence, she whispered, "Thanks."

"But we don't always have to win something to be a success—or happy," he pointed out. "Didn't we just teach Annabelle that?"

"I guess." She chuckled in self-deprecation. "It's just…" Her eyes became shiny, and Evan realized she was fighting tears. He looked back at the flames to give her privacy. "I miss Mia," she whispered. "We didn't talk much, but I always knew she was there. We just… The thing is," stammered Kylee, "she was a beautiful person. She had a lot of talent, and she was sweet, and everyone instantly loved her. She never met a stranger. She never had an enemy."

"I can attest to that," said Evan. "She adored you," he assured her.

Kylee grimaced. "I don't know."

"You're kidding."

She shook her head. "Mia was competitive, and so was I. A lot more."

"There's nothing wrong with that."

"I meant she was into sports. She loved the attention. For me, it's different."

"How so?"

Kylee paused. "I *have* to win. I can't bear second place." She let out a sudden, sharp laugh. "I guess Annabelle gets that from me."

Evan smiled. "Maybe. Why do you think you feel that way?"

"When Mia was born, she got all the attention. She was such a sunbeam. That never really changed."

"You were jealous," Evan said in surprise.

Kylee looked down at her hands. "Without realizing it," she insisted. "I mean, I guess I did, sometimes. I received the attention at school I wanted when I did better than every-one else, and of course my parents always praised my grades and academic pursuits. That's when I felt the most seen."

"So it drove you to become the best."

"I couldn't outdo everyone in gym class, so I... Well, academics was where I could outshine her, and deep down I thought it'd get me further. I thought if I became a huge success, I would be..." Kylee sighed.

"You wanted approval from your parents, that's all. It's natural."

"Sometimes I wonder. I was so busy trying to do better than everyone, was I a little too prideful about doing bet-ter than my own sister?" Kylee's eyes suddenly brimmed with tears. "Who does that?" she choked, staring at him directly as if he had an answer.

Evan realized cleaning out her sister's room had been

harder on Kylee than she'd expected. He covered her hand with his. "I never once heard Mia criticize you for pursuing a career and being so successful. She was super proud of you."

Kylee motioned toward the hall. "Mia always did her own thing and never worried about what anyone thought, and that was what made her special." Her voice cracked. "She played sports through high school, got her associate's degree, married her college sweetheart and had children because that's what she wanted to do. And everyone admired her for it. She's the true success."

Without thinking, Evan wound his arm behind Kylee's back and gave her a comforting squeeze. "In the end, we're all going to the same place," he reminded her. "We're traveling back to God but taking different paths, and that's how it's supposed to be. No one was meant to take the same road. It'd make us robots, without agency, and we'd never learn or grow. She chose her path. You chose yours. The only thing that matters in the end is how we treated others and who we became."

Kylee nodded, dabbing her eyes.

"She wasn't perfect, you know," teased Evan.

She looked at him in surprise. "Seriously? Mia?"

"Yes! She was a great friend and person, but she had her faults."

"Like what?" she demanded.

He motioned toward the kitchen. "She was messy. Total clutter bug. And she was late to everything." He laughed as memories washed over him. "It drove Chip crazy."

"She had no respect for other people's time," Kylee began, then she stopped herself as if she knew she sounded critical. "Well, no one's perfect," she murmured. "You're right."

"I know she was amazing, and I know you loved her."

Kylee dropped her head down. "I spent so many years being jealous of her, and then all of a sudden, she was gone, and it was too late."

Evan patted her hand. "In my line of work, I've seen a lot of people die and families suffer," he began. "I've also seen people be brave and find comfort in their beliefs. Faith is a part of healing, and if you believe in God and peace in the next life, then you have to believe it's never too late to be sorry and let things go."

Kylee lifted her chin in agreement as Evan studied her. "If your sister didn't love and trust you, she would have never asked you to take the twins. She wanted them to be happy and have a family. You are her sister. You are their family." He watched water well up in Kylee's eyes again. "Maybe she knew something you didn't."

Kylee gave Evan a meek smile. "I always prided myself on having more common sense, but I never realized she had more faith than me. That's something I need to work on."

Her confession astonished Evan, and he realized he'd been wrong about Kylee from the start. She was more humble and self-critical than he would have guessed. "Hey, it's never something you achieve perfectly. It's an ongoing process." He nudged her. "That's why going to church can be so important. You can be uplifted and inspired by others when you join in worship. It feeds faith in a way you just can't do on your own."

She wiped the corners of her eyes with a sigh. "I guess."

"I don't believe anyone is meant to be alone, Kylee," said Evan. When she met his gaze, his breath fluttered in his chest like leaves on the wind.

"In the end, I always am," Kylee murmured. "I've put success before anything and anyone else all my life, and I've always been on my own."

He slanted his head. "Well, you clearly love Annabelle and Henry, and I'd say you definitely know when to make allowances. You're here, and you're doing a good job. We just have different approaches."

"Thank you, Evan," she whispered.

He nodded, mesmerized by her soft cheeks. He felt a warmth in his heart. It made him feel nervous. Why? He eased his arm out from behind her back and leaned forward on his elbows, pretending to study the television. He'd been mistaken about her. But that didn't mean sitting close enough to her to smell her faint perfume and feel her warmth had to make him think about her in ways that went beyond admiration or respect.

He cleared his throat and saw the clock on the mantel was minutes away from striking nine. "I better get to work," he said, jarring the silence between them.

"Sure," she agreed quietly, looking straight ahead.

Another glance at the movie playing on the screen showed a couple standing under some mistletoe, and Evan resisted the urge to rush out of the house.

That was one thing that would never happen with Mia's sister. Right?

With the exception of tangled thoughts about the twins' godfather, Friday ran smoothly and Saturday morning almost felt like any other day, except Kylee was relieved at how nice it was not to have spent her week in an office. She made the twins scrambled eggs, satisfied they came out only dark brown and not black. Evan would have been impressed. He'd been so sweet and comforting after she packed up Mia's room, she'd had to admit the attraction she felt for him had depth. But that couldn't matter. She had work to do.

The next big task was laundry, which seemed to multiply like snowflakes. Only there was no snow outside because it was Georgia. Still, the twins did need jackets most days, and they weren't any better at keeping them clean than they were their clothes.

Kylee shoved as much dirty laundry as she could fit into the washer in the interest of time, since she'd promised to take the twins to Murphy's for a book if they cleaned their bedroom. After scrubbing down the bathroom, she checked on them and found they'd made little to no progress cleaning their room, but at least the bedding had come off as she requested. She dragged the sheets into the hall, and after considering how many more loads they'd make, she opened the lid to the churning top loader and stuffed them in. She slammed the lid shut to make sure it'd seal, then as an afterthought, opened it again and poured in more detergent.

"Aunt Kylee, we need help," Henry called from their room, and she trotted back down the hall.

There'd been no whining or fighting, and Henry at least wanted to make an effort to follow directions. Probably because he wanted a new book, but that was fine. She didn't mind seeing their bookshelf grow, and Evan didn't seem to mind reading to them. In fact, he relished it.

Kylee chuckled to herself as she helped Annabelle sort toys into the correct bins. Instituting a penalty box for toys left out in the living room had helped, but the picked-up items were usually tossed quickly into their bedroom and the door shut.

"Are you happy?" Annabelle asked suddenly. She tilted her head and eyed her aunt.

Kylee stopped with her hand in midair, clutching a building block. "What?"

"You're happy today."

"Why do you think that?" Kylee asked with curiosity.

"You're not grouchy," echoed Henry. He'd crawled under the bed and was throwing out random toy army men.

"I'm never grouchy," Kylee insisted.

"Sometimes you are," said Annabelle.

"Thanks a lot." Is that what they thought? That she was crabby? She didn't want to be the grumpy old aunt. They'd had a great night on Thursday, right? Evan had made them a delicious dinner, they'd played games and laughed and… Well, she'd cleaned out Mia's room, but she'd felt better once she returned to the children and Evan.

Her heart flipped. *Evan.* He'd comforted her on the couch. Listened to her talk through her feelings. He'd even squeezed her hand, cupping it into his big palms and making her feel safe, understood…and then his arm had gone around her and made her stomach drop. She was sure he was only being friendly. Mia had counted him as one of her closest friends, and not just because he and Chip grew up together. Mia trusted him. He was the twins' godfather, after all. That had to mean that Kylee could trust him as well. And she wanted to.

Kylee turned back to sorting the colored blocks, ignoring the fact that Annabelle had forgotten what they were supposed to be doing and was building something that looked like a prison tower. No doubt Evan would make up a story about it. "What are you building?"

"A giraffe."

"It's beautiful."

"I know it."

Kylee snorted.

Henry crawled up beside her. He had a miniature army man in one hand. "Here." He held out the toy. Kylee took the army man and dropped him into the action figure bin.

"Here," Henry repeated, and she looked down at a crumpled tissue in his hand.

"Ew."

"It was under my bed. You said to clean under the bed."

"You can go throw it away."

"Why?"

"Because I don't want your germs," she managed to say.

Henry grunted but army-crawled from the room. She watched his heels disappear out the door. Just as she dropped the last toy into a bin, minus Annabelle's giraffe project, Henry hollered from the hallway, "Oh no!"

Kylee stood up and wiped her hands on her jeans. They were sticky. *Reminder—clean the kids' toys.* Her brain raced, wondering how Mia had cleaned toys. She remembered the Barbie in the bathroom sink and glanced at the toy bins.

"Aunt Kylee!" Henry sounded unusually dramatic.

The bathtub, she thought, congratulating herself on her good idea. She could just dump everything into the tub to soak. She crossed her arms and surveyed the amount of toys. Nothing a little hot water couldn't handle.

"There's bubbles everywhere," Henry called.

Bubbles. Dish soap. That'd be perfect. Kylee nodded to herself. Could she put them into a dryer? It's not like anything would shrink.

Annabelle sashayed out of the room. "Bubbles!" she shrieked moments later, then broke into laughter.

"Aunt Kylee!" Henry's voice went up an octave.

Flustered, Kylee left the semi-clean bedroom, deciding it was good enough for the bookstore trip. When had she gotten to be an old softy?

Two steps out the bedroom, she was met with foam oozing out of the laundry closet's bifold doors. Seconds later, her feet landed in a puddle. She stopped and stared.

Annabelle scooped up a giant armful of suds and threw them into the air. "Snow!" she shouted, and Henry's panic turned to amusement. Then he spotted Kylee.

"I didn't do it," he exclaimed. He pointed at the laundry room closet. "They're coming from there."

Kylee realized there was a horrible squishing sound coming from the closet. It sounded like a hog grunting for air. Hog? Where had that come from? After almost twenty years in New York, was she already reverting to her Southern roots? She sloshed to the closet and yanked the doors open.

Bubbles flew everywhere. She stood ankle deep in them as they floated around. Annabelle raced up and down the hall giggling with glee, and Kylee sighed. She lifted the lid to the foaming washer and saw trillions of suds. Rotating the dial to Off, she swiped soap out of the way to find a giant knot of clothing and sheets. They were twisted around the agitator in wet ropes. She groaned. What would Mia say?

Regardless, they needed clean clothes for tomorrow if they were going to church. Kylee clenched her jaw. What was she going to do? There was no concierge service here in town.

"What a mess," Henry declared. He'd shown up with a mop like a little janitor, bless his heart. That was what she needed, she sighed. A janitor. And a laundromat.

Wait. They had laundromats in Georgia. There was no reason for Mom to find out about this; no reason for Evan to, either. She didn't want him to know. Not after he'd told her she was doing a good job.

"Thank you," she told Henry, taking the mop. "Go get

some towels from the bathroom. We'll have this cleaned up in no time."

And they did. It only took some problem-solving to figure out that the wet clothes and sheets could be taken to the laundromat in trash bags. After an early dinner, she packed the car up with the half-washed laundry, telling herself the twins would love to be pushed around in rolling baskets, and they'd surely be fascinated by the vending machines. And they'd forget all about the bookstore, and nobody would have to know she'd made such a ridiculous mistake.

Chapter Eight

On Sunday, Evan wondered if Kylee and the kids would attend Good Shepherd's services after their little talk. He got the impression she hadn't attended in a while and wondered if it was difficult in New York, or if she'd just become too busy. Maybe she was so independent she thought she didn't need God, but was he any better? When he attended services these days, he sat in the back or sulked. It was difficult to see his friends and neighbors there without Chip and Mia. His mom had started attending an old friend's congregation near the Alabama line, and that made it even more difficult to show up every Sunday. Now he was truly alone.

He arrived a few minutes early to find that Kylee and the twins were not there. Disappointed, he took a seat beside Tam Rochester while the Lightfoots headed to their preferred pew down front beside Monk Coles—everyone's favorite retired teacher and willing handyman.

Tam Rochester greeted Evan with a smile. "Did you work last night?"

"No, I'm off on weekends now." Tam was his longtime friend from the local herb shop. She always brought treats and herbal teas to the station on holidays and was good friends with Shawna. This year, she'd invited anyone who wished to come to her home for Thanksgiving.

"Get any sleep?" she asked in concern.

He lifted a shoulder. "Some." It'd been hard to sleep even on a shift break because he hadn't been able to quit thinking about Kylee. He could be honest with himself that he liked her, and he respected her, too. He'd seen the way she acted with the children when she sat between them after dinner on the couch. There was something more relaxed about her; she'd slowed down. And, he admitted, she'd quickly adapted from her role as a career woman to a full-time guardian.

Just as wiry, petite Sister Lovell began to pound on the organ, the pew creaked beneath him. Evan looked over to see the twins wriggling down the bench toward him. Henry grinned and climbed up beside him as Evan's mood soared. Kylee herded a grumbling Annabelle ahead of her and widened her eyes at Evan in an attempt to show her exasperation. She was only a few minutes late, but the children were dressed, and she looked…amazing.

Evan's heart flared around the edges like a kite catching the breeze. It was only gratitude that she'd finally brought the children to church, he told himself. Not the subtle makeup that accented her face, not her glossy, walnut-brown hair, or the orange-red sweater that made her skin glow, not to mention how it hugged her waist with a belt around it.

She sat down on the other side of Annabelle, and with the twins between them, Evan felt himself relax, as if he were complete.

A few moments later, the pastor began an interesting sermon on the background of the Savior's mission and purpose. After a resounding reading of the Beatitudes, Evan put his arm around Henry, who stood up on the pew to sing next to him in between yawns. Evan was impressed the boy knew the chorus, and when he glanced at Kylee to point it out, their eyes met. She smiled, then shifted her gaze around the room.

After the song and the closing prayer, the worshippers quickly broke into friendly conversations. Before Evan could inquire about Kylee's morning, Tam tapped her shoulder from the other side. "No playgroup this Tuesday," she reminded her. "It's turkey week!"

"Yes, I know," said Kylee.

"What are you doing for Thanksgiving?" Evan blurted when she grinned.

Tam chirped, "You should come to my house! We're eating in the late afternoon so Evan and any of his coworkers can join us."

He nodded, watching Kylee's expression for any hint of mulishness. She looked relieved. "I suppose we could. Mom is going out of town."

"She mentioned that," said Evan.

"She's going to my uncle Tim's house in Dothan. His health is not great, and I don't want to stress him out with too many visitors." Kylee's cheeks flushed, but she nodded at Tam. "I'm sure the twins would appreciate it. What can I bring?"

"Nothing!" answered Tam a little too fast, and Kylee's gaze darted to Evan.

He held up his hands. "I didn't say anything."

"About what?" Tam wondered aloud.

"I don't cook much," admitted Kylee, sounding somewhat disgruntled.

Tam laughed. "Oh, that. Mia told me once, but that's not why I said that." She elbowed Evan. "Although, he did tell us about the tuna casserole, so I figured it wasn't your forte."

Kylee gave Evan a side-eye, then grinned. "It was pretty bad."

"I hate tuna," said Annabelle.

"Well, now you do," Kylee returned.

"We'll be having turkey and potatoes and stuffing on Thanksgiving. You'll love it," Tam promised. "Gretchen will bring her family, and Ali will be there with her husband, son and baby girl."

Kylee smiled. "Great. I'll see you all there."

Tam promised to text her the address, then waved goodbye and exited the row with her daughter, Piper, both of them disappearing into the crowd.

Henry and Annabelle crawled under the pew to escape, but Kylee called, "Don't go any farther than you can see me, or there will be no playtime today." She leaned back onto the bench with a sigh.

Evan was suddenly reluctant to leave. "I guess I'll see you Tuesday then?"

"Yes, thanks. It's been a crazy weekend sorting out Mia's room on top of everything else."

Evan realized there were a few waves in her usually straightened hair. The collar of the shirt she wore beneath her sweater was a little rumpled, much like the twins' outfits. "Well, at least you made it here."

"Barely. Annabelle said it was too cold to get out, but we managed to peel her from the car seat."

"She'll get the hang of it before you know it." Evan looked out the window where the foliage had thinned. Any lingering leaves were brown, orange or the occasional burst of red. "After a sermon and then an hour of Sunday School, I think they'll be ready to settle down for lunch and rest time."

"I hope so," she replied. "I have tons of laundry to fold."

"It's Sunday." Evan scooted down beside her. "Work can always wait. Take a breather."

"I guess I'm not used to doing that. Although that's something I've missed. Sundays. Potlucks…" She waved her arm toward the pulpit, and he knew what she really meant. She missed God.

Annabelle crawled next to his shoes on the floor and looked up at him.

"You're going to get dirty down there," he scolded her. "And make more laundry for Aunt Kylee."

"I like laundry," Annabelle sang, her disheveled head bobbing up and down. "We put quarters in the machine and got candy."

Evan wrinkled his brow and shot a curious look at Kylee.

She shrugged. "We had a little trouble with the washing machine yesterday. So we went to the laundromat last night."

"The laundromat?" repeated Evan in surprise. "Why didn't you call me?"

"Oh, no, you've done enough," she insisted. "Besides, you were off work."

Evan frowned. He would have gone anyway. "You could have used my machine."

She waved him off. "It's fine, Evan. I handled it, without bothering you or my mother."

"By taking them to a laundromat at night?"

"We were home by nine, and Annabelle fell asleep in a laundry basket anyway."

Evan tamped down a flicker of irritation. "All you had to do was call for help."

"I don't call for help," Kylee reminded him. "I figure out how to do things myself, remember?"

"Mmm." She had surprised him, but Evan had to resist

mentioning his macaroni and cheese. What had happened to the washing machine? At his knee, Annabelle let out a barking cough. "It sounds like she's coming down with something."

Kylee's soft jawline tightened as if someone had jerked a string. "She's fine, Evan."

"I'll come over and look at the washer today."

"No need. I have a number to call for service. It's under control," Kylee assured him.

"That's a lot of money to spend if there's just a toy lodged in it."

"There's not a toy," she insisted. "It just…gave out. It's not my fault the washing machine can't handle a big load."

"There were bubbles everywhere," supplied Annabelle. She got up to her feet and waved her arms in the air. "It was snowing bubbles!"

Kylee's cheeks turned red.

"You overstuffed it," guessed Evan.

"I didn't know that was possible. It says it's heavy-duty."

"That doesn't mean it doesn't have a limit." Evan squeezed his eyes shut. He could only imagine the condition of the washing machine.

"Time to go," Kylee said sharply. She rose to her feet, pulling her handbag over her shoulder.

Evan shook his head. All he wanted was to help, and all she needed to do was ask. He stood up as well. "I wish you would have called me," he told her.

"I will when I need you," she said without missing a beat.

"I'm hungry," Annabelle announced.

"Henry!" snapped Kylee. The boy was standing at the window touching a piece of blue stained glass. "See you Tuesday," she said to Evan.

He didn't reply. In the firehouse, everyone had an assignment, but they also watched out for each other. Even a fire chief knew when to call in another station if the flames were more than his company could handle alone.

Evan walked out of the church. Someday Kylee was going to need somebody, and he hoped he was there to help when she did.

The phone call to the washing machine repair place did not go as planned on Monday because everyone was on vacation for Thanksgiving, so Kylee made an appointment for the following week. Because the laundry basket was already somehow overflowing, and she was expecting Mom to stop by later that day, Kylee just piled everything into the laundry closet and closed the doors.

It was frustrating that Evan had been upset at her for washing their clothes at the laundromat. Yes, it'd been late for the children and had cost quite a chunk of change, but she'd had no other choice. She hadn't wanted to bother him while he was off work, and she certainly wouldn't have bothered Mom in the evening, since she needed her rest. They had both done so much already. She wanted them to see she could carry her load.

Both Annabelle and Henry were crabby today, too, which made it even harder to finish emptying out the last of Mia's closet. The boxes of shoes and random accessories seemed so final, Kylee worried she might not be able to handle the arrival of the charity truck. Packing up framed pictures was difficult enough, but getting rid of Chip's and Mia's clothes felt like she was erasing their very existence.

Annabelle coughed in the next room, and Kylee cringed. The little girl had not taken her jacket to the laundromat, and unless one stood near the commercial dryers, the room had been cold. Perhaps running around and touching every surface had not been the best idea, either.

Just then the doorbell rang, and Kylee bristled. "Do not color on anything but paper," she warned Annabelle, who was at the kitchen table coloring with her brother.

It wasn't the charity truck but her mother.

"How are you, dear?" Mom wrapped her in a big hug. "I'm leaving for Dothan this afternoon and wanted to make sure you were all okay."

"I'm fine," fibbed Kylee.

Mom saw the neatly taped boxes in the foyer. "I see you finished going through her room."

"Yes," admitted Kylee, noting Mom had not been able to voice Mia's name. "They should be coming to pick them up soon."

As if reading her mind, Mom said, "I'm sure Evan can take them if they don't show up."

"Yes, I'm sure he wouldn't mind," Kylee relented. He was so thoughtful and eager to help, she knew she could ask him.

Stepping into the kitchen, Mom draped her arms around Henry's shoulders. His head was bent over his coloring book as he scribbled furiously with a bright green crayon. "That's beautiful, honey," she whispered. She cocked her head to look at Kylee, who hoped she didn't notice the sink was stacked with dishes.

"When you see Evan, would you tell him someone from Martin Tanner's office called me?" Mom requested. "They asked a lot of questions." She seemed mildly concerned.

"Who's Martin Tanner?" Kylee wondered aloud.

"A local lawyer," said Mom. She pulled out a chair between the twins and sat down.

Kylee felt a prickle of concern. "Is everything okay?"

"Hmm? Oh, yes." Mom picked up a crayon and began to color on a ripped-out coloring page. Annabelle stopped to watch her with interest. "He just wanted to know what I thought of you being here and how things were going."

Something like alarm crept up Kylee's spine. "Why would he want to know that?"

"I imagine because Evan considered seeking custody of the twins when he realized how much worse my fibromyalgia had become and that you needed some time before coming home."

The burning fingers tapping Kylee's back turned into an icy cold grip. "I didn't know that." Evan wasn't the type to betray another person, was he?

"He wanted to take them immediately, but they're my grandchildren, and I knew he wasn't ready to raise two children on his own without time to make arrangements. We worked things out until—"

"I got here," Kylee finished. She felt ill. Had she misjudged the handsome paramedic?

"Well, yes," agreed Mom, casting her a confused look. "I think he had some doubts you would accept custody. He wants to continue to be a part of their lives no matter what happens, so maybe that's why Mr. Martin called."

It all made sense. The constant checking in. Intervening. Helping out. Evan not only wanted to be the twins' favorite, but he was also positioning himself to take over as their guardian. He was plotting to take them away, to stop her from taking her own niece and nephew back to New York where they would have a better life.

He wanted her to fail. Did he really care about her at all? She realized with a start, she cared about him.

Pain and betrayal began to fill up her chest. "What's going to happen is I'm going to take them back to New

York for Christmas," said Kylee a little too loudly. "And they're going to be happy and just fine."

"I want to go to New York!" cried Annabelle, always afraid of missing a party.

"You will, sweetheart," Kylee soothed her. She circled the table and wrapped her arms about the little girl. "And you're going to love it. They have real snow and giant toy stores and even ice-skating in the middle of the city. There's even going to be a big gingerbread house contest, too."

Annabelle's eyes glazed over. "Ohhh!"

Kylee glanced at Henry. He was wearing the green crayon down to a nub coloring in St. Nick's toy sack on the page.

Finishing her picture of a reindeer, Mom climbed to her feet. "Well, I wanted to see if you needed any help before I left for Thanksgiving, but it looks like you have everything under control."

"Oh, I do," said Kylee, now seething. "Believe me, I do." She could hardly wait to call *her* lawyer and inform him of the possible custody battle.

Her mind raced through her to-do list as her mother let herself out. The nanny service in New York had already gotten back to her, and interviews would start after the holidays. She could work from home with the twins in the apartment until after the new year. It'd give them time to acclimate to their new city.

She gave Annabelle another insecure squeeze. "It's time to play outside," she announced, glad they'd eaten their lunch. "And you, young lady, are going to wear a coat."

"No, I'm not," said Annabelle.

"I will," Henry assured her.

"I will, too," Annabelle decided, flipping sides. "And I'll wear my boots," she added to outdo her brother.

Kylee returned to the dishes in the sink, giving her niece a fleeting glance. The little girl's profile jolted Kylee's heart. Annabelle was nothing like her mother, she realized, because she was so much like her aunt.

Chapter Nine

Evan raised his fist to knock on the door of the twins' house Tuesday afternoon, but hesitated. Martin had called him that morning with an update. Kylee's custody was being finalized. It'd filled him with concern, but he'd already decided: washing machines or not, the twins did belong with Kylee. Despite her stubbornness, she was efficient, organized, and she loved them. He knew it. And he didn't want to be fighting against Chip and Mia's final wishes. Besides, it was none of his business where she washed their clothes. He knew she'd never put the kids in harm's way if she could help it. There was no use raising her ire. Besides, Tanner had told him that actually gaining custody didn't look like a possibility. There was nothing dark or sinister, much less concerning, in Kylee's past.

Taking them to New York was not child endangerment, and with her high-powered career, she'd be able to afford to give them a lot more than he ever could. He still wished he could make her understand that having him in their lives was better than fancy private schools and that the most important thing was family. But she was their closest living relative, not him, even if she didn't think Lagrasse was good enough.

He braced himself and rapped on the door. After a few moments, he heard scuffling. It opened slowly. "Hi," he said.

Kylee turned on her heel without a word and returned to the kitchen, and he heard the rustle of her purse and keys.

"Where are the twins?" he asked when he realized he was at a loss for anything more to say.

"They're under the bed with flashlights and jelly beans," she informed him.

"Jelly beans?"

"Old Easter candy from Mia's closet. Seemed a shame to throw it out."

"I didn't know she liked jelly beans."

"Apparently she hoarded them," said Kylee. "Big secret." Her tone sounded accusing.

"Is everything okay?"

Ignoring his query, she said, "Other than risking diabetes and cavities, the twins are ready for reading time. But you can handle anything, right?"

"I guess." Evan's gut twisted. "Look, I really am sorry about overreacting about the laundromat. I'm a bit overprotective, I know, but—"

"You think? Or are you just a better option than me?"

"What?"

She jerked her purse strap onto her shoulder. "I hear you have a lawyer."

"Oh. I, ah…" Evan stammered. His thoughts blurred. "Yeah. I mean, I needed help because I was their emergency contact after your mom. And she's…"

"Fragile, I know," said Kylee. Suspicion darkened her features. "Why are you still in contact with him now?"

"Well, I wasn't sure you'd want custody, but it seems you're getting it."

"Am I?" He stared at her for too long, and she blurted,

"Why do you need to meet with your lawyer and why is he asking my mom questions about me?"

"I'm not your enemy. There's no need to interrogate me. I just wanted to learn more about the custody arrangement."

"I think you mean hostile takeover."

"No." Evan shook his head. "No, I just…"

"You just what?"

He felt his jaw tighten and put his hands on his hips. "Well, obviously, Kylee, I thought I was the better option for the kids."

"You what?"

He nodded as if it would convince her. "You want to go back to New York."

"Yes. So?"

"But Lagrasse is their home."

"They'll have a new one."

"Maybe they don't want to go. Have you asked them?"

"They're children," she hissed. "I'm in charge of what's best for them. They aren't old enough to make that decision."

"Are you sure?"

"Yes. I am. If I thought they absolutely had to stay here to flourish or to be happy, I would stay." A black storm swirled in her brown eyes.

"I thought I should be ready in case you decided you couldn't handle this," Evan explained.

She jabbed a finger in his direction. "You think I can't handle it?"

"I didn't say that."

"Oh, no? What about showing up for their playgroup? Cooking? Checking up on their schedule?"

"I think you've proved you can do anything if you put your mind to it. I just wanted to be ready to make that sacrifice if you weren't," replied Evan.

"Well, kindly inform your lawyer you don't need him anymore. I'm not giving up my rights to raise these children, and I am taking them to New York before Christmas."

"Before?" He scowled. "What happened to after? We have the Nativity pageant."

"I never said after. I'll get to show them the wonders of Christmas in New York. The Christmas tree at Rockefeller Center. Ice-skating in Central Park."

Evan took a deep breath and counted to five in his head before speaking. She couldn't take them before the Nativity. She just couldn't. "I'm sure it would be an adventure, but..."

She gave him a quiet stare. "I should go. I have an appointment at the bank to close out Mia and Chip's account, and don't worry, it's going into the trust fund. I won't spend it."

"I didn't think you were, and I wouldn't blame you if you did," said Evan, confused.

"I just wanted you to know so you could keep your lawyer informed," Kylee replied with a tinge of accusation.

Evan felt his face warm with guilt. "I meant to tell you..."

"That you've only been helping out to spy on me?"

"What? No!" There were so many other reasons. He cared about her. A lot. But she wouldn't want to hear that right now.

"To take my job? Take the twins?" she continued.

"No, it's not like that," he returned, feeling defensive.

"It seems like you've had every intention of fighting me for custody of the children since the day I arrived. Probably since the reading of the will."

Evan held up a hand. "Look," he began.

"No, you look," she said, sounding just like Annabelle. "I promised you a few hours a week with them, and I'm going to hold up my end of the bargain until the custody hearing."

The heavy pain Evan had carried for so long found its way out before he could stop it. "I was there with Chip and Mia. Me. At the scene of the accident. I had to see them, and I have to carry those memories with me for the rest of my life because I couldn't save them. Of course I want to do everything I can for their children."

Kylee took a step back, her shoulders drooping. There was a quiet, uncomfortable pause. Then she said, "I'm sorry. I'm glad someone was there when they passed." She dropped her eyes to the floor. "But you had a lawyer. All this time. Because you thought that I wasn't good enough to raise Mia and Chip's children."

Evan slanted his head, imploring her to understand. "Your mom said she'd support me if you decided not to take custody. She loves you, Kylee. Don't you see that?"

"She knew about it, and you're defending her?"

Evan recoiled. Kylee had pain and anger inside of her that was misdirected. "You'll go after anything you want, but have you ever asked your family for what you needed?"

"No. Mia got it all," she mumbled.

Evan stiffened. "I know she wasn't my sister, but I knew her well enough to know if she was aware that you felt that way, she would have done something about it."

"Of course she would have."

"Kylee, it's not a contest." Evan huffed. It seemed like the Spokeses had inadvertently showered Mia with more affection than their elder daughter, or at least she thought so. And rather than speak up, Kylee had compensated by overachieving. "Let me ask you a question," he said. "If you had children and knew you'd pass away, would you have left them in her care?"

Kylee crossed her arms. "Yes, of course."

"Because you trusted her," he said. "Because you loved her, and deep down in your heart, you know she loved you, too."

Kylee pressed her lips together and studied the floor. After a moment, she said, "I'll be back later and bring some groceries." Her tone was as cool as the blustery wind outside. She hurried past him, and Evan resisted the urge to reach out for her arm, to touch her, to make her understand.

"It was only because I didn't think you would take them with your career and all," he blurted after her. "You came home so little. I didn't think you'd want them."

With her hand on the doorknob, she turned to face him. Hysterical giggles echoed from the twins' bedroom down the hall. Glorious, happy, innocent sounds. Evan's heart sank when he saw Kylee's eyes glisten.

"The charity came by and picked up Chip's and Mia's things. I forgot to ask for a receipt, so I have to go grab that, too. Don't worry about me for dinner." She gave him another long look, then added, "And I do want them. They love me. I love them. And I'm good enough." She said it defiantly, and although he was frustrated and desperate for her to understand, he admired her for it.

"Then they're yours," Evan answered, instead of telling her how happy he was that she'd decided to keep them. But he'd do anything to change her mind about taking them to New York.

"I know," she said. "So please, tell your lawyer to lay off."

Wednesday was quiet, but Kylee was sure she was going to get an ulcer between keeping up with the holidays, work and backup plans in the event her custody of the twins became a fight. Evan had stabbed her in the back just like someone in her fast-paced marketing world would do. She should have expected it.

But despite being gutted at Evan's betrayal, Kylee decided she would hold her head up and go to Tam's Thanksgiving dinner anyway. Even though she couldn't help but wonder how many people knew he'd been plotting to stop her from raising the twins all along. The worst thing was that it went against her sister's wishes.

She'd found a worn cookbook in the pantry. Her heart tugged at the red-and-white gingham cover she knew had been treasured by her grandmother, mother and sister. She found the slow-cooker recipes especially interesting; she was rather nostalgic when it came to Mom's roast, potatoes and cabbage that had seemed to magically appear every Sunday afternoon. The robust flavors made the house smell wonderful, her mouth watering as soon as she walked in the door after Sunday School. And then there were the biscuits.

Kylee snorted to herself. Her baking skills were a long way off from making biscuits, but Mia had left handwritten notes in the margins for several recipes. Feeling brave, Kylee decided she would take cranberry sauce to Tam's for Thanksgiving dinner after all. The berries had been easy to find at the store, and the other ingredients were simple. She'd measured the spices, looked up what zesting an orange meant, and after figuring out which kitchen tools to use, mixed everything up, turned the slow cooker on Low and let it cook overnight, hoping it would not burn.

The next morning, Thanksgiving Day, the house smelled delicious. The twins were excited to go see Ava and Tyler and eat turkey, and seemingly hadn't made the painful connection between last Thanksgiving with their parents and this, their first one without them. Still, Kylee was incredibly pleased at how the cranberry sauce turned out, and when she arrived at Tam's modest house on Church Street, she proudly carried in the dish with the twins dancing behind her in their best clothes. The outfits were a wee bit small, but she'd somehow managed to squeeze the kids into them. She'd made a note in her Reminders app that it was time for new clothes for the twins.

Tam's mouth dropped open when she lifted the lid of the slow cooker and looked inside. She put a hand on her hip. "Did you buy this at the deli and dump it in or make it from scratch?"

Kylee grinned at her. "I made it myself. I'm not that useless, you know."

"I never thought you were," said Tam, impressed. She motioned toward the family room. "Come on in. There's deviled eggs and cheese and crackers in the other room, and the game is on."

Kylee wasn't sure what game she meant, but she knew Evan would likely be in there. She took a deep breath, but before leaving asked, "Did you know Evan had a lawyer?"

"Hmm?" Tam stopped stirring a pot of corn on the stove and looked up with curiosity in her eyes.

"He had a lawyer checking into how I'm doing with the twins."

Seemingly nonplussed, Tam shrugged. "He hired him when your mom asked him for help taking care of them and making immediate decisions. You know, until you could get down here. She didn't want to bother you about details."

"Right," said Kylee. "But he wanted custody."

Her new friend put it together. "Kylee," she soothed her. "He didn't know if you'd agree to come down or not. He wanted to make sure he was ready. I don't know why the lawyer was asking around about you, but why don't you ask Evan yourself?"

"I did." Kylee gave her a tight smile, feeling her cheeks flush. No one had expected her to come. To show up. To care. And why should they have? She'd kept her distance and hadn't been there for a lot of things. Why would anyone expect her to be here now? "I hope you like the cranberry sauce." She sighed. "It's Mia's recipe."

"I can't wait." Tam winked at her.

Kylee exhaled quietly with relief. Dinner was sure to be delicious, but the cranberry sauce would be divine. Thanks to Mia and the recipe she'd left behind.

She eased into the living room, sensing Evan before she saw him, and hugged Monk Coles and his wife, Angie, before taking a seat. It felt like there was an empty space beside her, and she told herself it was because Mom had gone to Dothan, not because the twins had gone to play, leaving her alone. And not because Evan stayed on the other side of the room staring at the television and chatting with everyone else around him like she wasn't there.

When Chase had admitted to the crew on the night shift that he had nowhere to go for Thanksgiving, Evan had texted Tam to see if he could bring him along on late notice. It was just a few blocks south of the firehouse to her 1960s brick bungalow with white painted trim. The front yard was modest, but a glimpse into the back behind the separate garage showed an enormous garden with some herbs still leafy and green.

Evan shifted uncomfortably on the couch when Chase elbowed him as Kylee and the twins came into the house. The children darted off to play. Evan avoided eye contact with Kylee by staring at the football game on TV, but his partner shot to his feet to greet her and shake her hand.

From across the room, Tam waved for everyone's attention. "Dinner will be ready in a bit. Who wants spinach-and-artichoke dip?" Several hands went up.

Kylee was sitting on a straight-backed chair from the dining room, her legs crossed as she surveyed the room. When Annabelle came down the hall searching for her, her aunt held her on her lap all of three seconds before the little girl spotted Evan and climbed down.

"Uncle Evan!" she cheered.

Kylee gave him a searching stare as he opened his arms for the little girl to climb into his lap. He clutched Annabelle like a lifesaver. Her head leaned against his chest, and he felt his heart warm as he wrapped her in his arms.

Kylee got up and disappeared into the kitchen.

The younger children in the house played in the next room while older kids were scattered around the living room staring at their electronic devices. When Tam shooed Kylee out of the kitchen, Kylee saw that Ali's son had taken her chair. After an awkward pause, she sat down beside Evan.

"How's your week been?" he asked politely as he stared at the TV.

"Fine."

"I'm glad you made it to dinner."

"It's your afternoon to have them anyway."

"I appreciate that. I would have brought them here," Evan admitted.

"I figured as much, but Tam insisted that I come."

"Have you heard from your mom?"

"She dropped by just before she left town," Kylee replied. "It's supposed to storm down that way."

"Hopefully it won't here."

"Snow would be better," mused Evan.

"That doesn't happen here," Kylee reminded him. "It's one of the perks of living in New York."

Evan raised a brow. "I didn't know you liked snow so much."

"I love it. It's clean and quiet and makes everything in the city slow down."

"So you do like to slow down sometimes," he teased.

He thought he saw her stiffen. "When it's appropriate."

"It's Thanksgiving, and also, you're in Lagrasse. I hope you don't feel rushed here."

"Just on guard," she said under her breath.

He resisted the urge to reach for her hand like he had the night she cleaned her sister's room. "You don't have to be on guard here," he reassured her. "You're among friends."

"Right."

"You don't," he murmured.

"Quit flirting and watch the game," Chase chimed in.

Mortified, Evan felt his face warm. He cleared his throat at the attention, then tried to calm his pounding heart.

Kylee gave a small smile, but Evan saw her leg shaking back and forth. Every now and then, she'd look down the hall with her head inclined to listen for her niece and nephew. They were all that mattered to her right now, Evan realized. She was not on her phone. Or smoothing down her skirt. Or playing with her hair.

"I'm really sorry," blurted Evan in a hushed tone. "I should have mentioned Martin Tanner to you."

She remained silent, but her restless leg stilled.

"I know you're doing the best you can, and it's more than enough. Mia would be proud of you."

Kylee gave him a sideways glance. "Even without a washing machine?"

He bit the inside of his cheek. "Yeah. Even without a washer. Were you able to get in touch with a repair person?"

She shook her head. "No available appointments this week."

"You're welcome to use mine," he began.

"It's fine. I can use Mom's laundry room," said Kylee.

"Right." That made more sense. With a start, Evan realized Kylee didn't need him as much as he'd hoped she would. He'd noticed the slow cooker she'd carried into the kitchen.

"I see you're cooking now?" he probed. She'd figured out how to keep the house mostly clean despite the twins, and now she'd discovered slow cookers?

Suddenly there was a screech, and Kylee scooted back from her chair. "I'm trying." She hurried down the hall to investigate the cause of Annabelle's shrieks. Within seconds, the house quieted, but only for a moment.

"Dinner!" called Tam from the dining room, which was crammed with food and chairs. "Just wait until you try the cranberries," Tam gloated as everyone filed into the dining room. "Kylee outdid herself."

Evan's mouth watered, but he still felt oddly out of sorts. Was it Kylee? If he was honest with himself, the twins were safe and content, and he shouldn't get in the way. If he really wanted what was best for them, he'd take a step back and let them bond with their aunt, who would soon be taking them away from what could have been a painful Christmas. Instead, she could make it a special one, with lights and snow and gingerbread men in the big, bright city. But that meant that the upcoming holiday would be dismal for him, because the children—and now their aunt—had filled a room in his heart he hadn't realized was there.

Chapter Ten

❧

The next day, Kylee was torn between enjoying a day alone with the twins after so much socializing on Thanksgiving and missing one of her favorite events—Black Friday shopping. But she had to admit she found it more comfortable to stay home in her pajamas and shop online while Henry and Annabelle played around the house. She couldn't resist buying some Christmas lights to decorate the cottage for the holidays, even if she had to leave them behind when they moved to New York.

As if reading her thoughts, an email popped up from the Montessori school on the Upper East Side. The twins had been accepted into the prestigious preschool. A recommendation from her company's CEO had surely helped.

A storm that came in from the Gulf released torrents of water on Lagrasse over the next two days, and by Sunday, Kylee was sick of leftover turkey and rain and ready to go to church. She had not heard a peep from Evan, who'd said nothing about her excellent cranberry sauce. He actually hadn't stayed long after Thanksgiving dinner, claiming he and Chase had to get back to the firehouse. It stung a little that he hadn't said goodbye to her or the twins.

A part of her could now understand and even appreciate why he had been speaking with a lawyer. There was no reason not to accept his apology. He'd even offered her the use of his washing machine. So it was fine, she told herself, that the children needed him. She could not do character voices without feeling ridiculous, and Henry didn't help matters when she pulled out a Dr. Seuss book and he told her he was bored before she even got to Cindy Lou Who.

After the general meeting, Kylee dropped the children off at their Sunday School class and slipped into her own. Her mood rose when she saw a free seat beside Evan, Ali and her husband, Heath. She scooted into their row, clutching Mia's old Bible that had belonged to their father. It was well used, both of their writing familiar in the margins. There was something about seeing Dad's and Mia's thoughts that made them feel close by.

Kylee sat down next to Evan, who seemed surprised to see her, then looked away. In a lull of classroom conversation about the angel appearing to Zechariah to deliver God's promise for a son, Kylee folded her arms over the Bible and said in a low tone, "Henry does not like my version of the Grinch."

"I'm sure he'll get used to it," said Evan in a civil tone.

He looked nice, though a little fatigued, in a burgundy-checked dress shirt and gray slacks. His hair was beginning to curl around his ears and at the nape of his neck. Evan was a good man, inside and out. She'd been wrong to jump to conclusions about him and his intentions. Her old hypercompetitiveness had blinded her. "How was this weekend?" she asked. She wanted to offer an olive branch. She desperately wanted him to accept it.

He clasped his hands in his lap. "Fine," he whispered back.

She struggled for something more to say, desperate for the camaraderie they'd recently shared. She didn't plan to keep the twins away from him, but she did plan to keep guardianship of them. How could she make him understand? "I guess you're looking forward to Tuesday." She kept her voice low so as not to interrupt the class.

"For what?"

"Your shift with the twins," she said, trying to sound like she was teasing.

"Oh." He looked down at his Bible. The pages were creased and somewhat dog-eared.

"I guess I could do some Christmas shopping," Kylee admitted.

He glanced at her. "Did you know they're having a picnic at the park on Tuesday? The last one of the year. It's going to be around noon—the warmest part of the day. And it's supposed to be sunny."

"That sounds nice."

"You should go with the twins. I can meet you there, but only if you need me to," he added quickly.

She didn't need him to, but she wanted him there, Kylee realized. "I think the twins would enjoy seeing you."

"If it'll make them happy, I'll come by," he said. A few heads turned at the sound of their conversation, and Kylee flushed and sealed her lips shut.

It was evident that Evan would only be there for Henry and Annabelle. No matter how polite he was to her, it all came down to the twins. And that was how it should be, she told herself. But she liked how he made her feel he'd be there for her, too. It made being back home feel like…home.

"And after those days his wife Elisabeth conceived," read the teacher, "and hid herself five months, saying, Thus hath the Lord dealt with me in the days wherein he looked on me, to take away my reproach among men."

Kylee scanned the verses in the book open before her.

Elisabeth had been blessed at an incredible and improbable time in her life. In the same way, Kylee's niece and nephew were gifts—from her sister and God. So why was she letting the paramedic distract her from the two new and most important things in her life? And why did he make her feel like this was where she belonged when New York was waiting?

Evan had an emergency call during his Monday night shift that left him drained the next morning. The small kitchen fire in the victim's home had quickly spread and consumed the house, allowing its occupants to barely escape. Had he arrived earlier, he told himself, worked harder, he may have helped spare the house, but it was too late. He felt dejected knowing a family had lost everything. Even with Chase, Shawna and the rest of their team beside him, the fire had been unstoppable. After sleeping a few troubling hours at the firehouse, he'd dragged himself home and washed up.

Still, he'd been unable to forget the invitation to the playground picnic. It niggled at him a little bit, and he wasn't sure why. Perhaps it was because the only hope he had to keep the twins in his life was to convince Kylee to stay in town. Besides the children, her mom needed her, too. But for her to stay meant feeling whatever was stirring between them. There was no use avoiding her if he wanted to spend his last remaining weeks with the children, so he threw on a thick sweatshirt and headed for the park. He'd offered to bring lunch for all of them, but she'd refused.

He found a swarm of children on the playground equipment and several parents chatting on benches or sprawled out on blankets. Ali and Kylee were sharing a bag of potato chips while relaxing on a thick wool blanket that had been spread on the ground. He gave a small wave, then stuck his hands in his pockets as Ali stood up. "Trooper! Get back here!" she called. "My dog," she explained in exasperation to him, then darted off after the dog with her infant cradled to her chest in a carrier.

"Evan!" shouted Annabelle from the top of a slide.

He turned and watched her slide down to the bottom. She dashed over to him and threw her arms around his legs in a tangled hug, then headed back to the playground, calling for Henry.

Evan gave Kylee a sideways glance. She'd rolled up the chip bag and was dusting off her hands.

"Hey," he called to her.

She pointed at a rolled-up newspaper. "I read about the fire last night."

He nodded and stepped closer to the blanket, and she motioned beside her. "Sit down. You must be tired."

"Hi, Evan," called one of the other mothers.

He lifted a hand in greeting before sitting down beside Kylee and stretching out his legs.

"Are you okay?" she asked.

"Yes," he said. "I just didn't sleep much."

"You didn't have to come, you know."

"I wanted to, and I told the kids I'd be here."

"Then I'm glad you made it. They're funny about people keeping their word. If I even hint I'm thinking about doing something, they hold me to it."

"They need that constant assurance in their life right now."

She gave him a sympathetic look. "Is the family from last night okay?"

"Other than losing everything they own, yes. No one at the station was hurt, either."

"Then it's a win."

He looked at her. "But they lost everything."

"They have their lives because of you and your team. I doubt they're concerned about their material things. Gratitude is funny like that."

Evan nodded slowly, realizing she could teach him a thing or two. "I'm glad no one was injured. I just wish I could have done more."

She made a soft noise, her eyes trained on the children dotting the playground. "It must be hard being a hero."

"What's that supposed to mean?"

She put a hand on her chest. "I know I'm a perfectionist, but I don't expect to be able to save the day all the time. We just do the best we can. I think you do your very best. I know how much you've done for the twins."

Her words struck him hard. "Sometimes your best isn't enough."

Henry ran over and plopped down beside them on the blanket. "I'm tired," he announced.

"Hey, champ." Evan put an arm around him. "Are you done already?"

"I wanna snack."

Kylee opened a traditional picnic basket, and Evan wondered where she found it. "That's nice. Mia always brought things in plastic bags," he said.

Kylee looked at him. "I picked this up at Brook's." She handed the boy a plastic container that he opened, and Evan saw it was filled with sliced apples, nuts and cheese. He raised a brow. "I've tried to move them away from peanut butter and jelly for a while," she admitted.

"The horror," he said, teasing, and she laughed.

Henry munched for a few minutes, then shared his raisins with Evan. Satisfied after coaxing Evan to try an almond, Henry crawled to his feet and wandered back toward the swings.

"I don't feel guilty for not feeding them peanut butter all the time," she said. "I thought it might be better to try to get some fruits and vegetables in their diet."

"I'm glad they don't have peanut allergies. I've seen some scary reactions. In some cases, help doesn't come soon enough. So I was super careful the first time I gave it to them. I didn't want that on my conscience."

Kylee slanted her head. "Mia gave them nuts all the time. You do so much for these kids. Is that why? Guilt?"

Evan stared straight ahead to hide the fact she'd made his nerves twinge—a pain that traveled straight to his heart. The December sky was a rich shade of blue, shimmering on the edges of indigo with streaks of white clouds.

"I mean, it wasn't your fault," she continued.

"I was there and didn't do enough," he blurted, startled at the punch he felt in his gut when he said it out loud. He glanced at her while forcing himself to maintain control. The last thing he wanted was to cry in front of her. "I wasn't fast enough. I didn't have the right equipment. I couldn't… couldn't…" He choked on grief that crept up his throat.

"You couldn't save them," she said. "No one could, and no one blames you for that."

Despite her generosity, Evan's chest felt like it was being squeezed by a vise. He concentrated on his breathing, a sharp pain swelling his heart. "They were my best friends, and I couldn't save them. The last thing Mia said to me was…" He gulped for air, feeling Kylee's keen stare. "The last she said was, *the babies*." He gulped. "I knew what she meant—who she meant."

"That's why you're doing this."

"I would have done it anyway," Evan insisted.

"Chip died instantly?"

"Yes, but she held on for a few minutes. If only I would have..." A desperate, raging sob inside him threatened to escape, and the world seemed to darken. Evan wanted to tuck his head between his knees, but he took a deep breath and let it out carefully.

"I know you tried everything to save my sister, Evan," said Kylee in a choked voice. She reached for his hand and held it tight. "Everyone says you're the best paramedic in the county. I never once thought..."

He took a deep breath and straightened, blinking in the golden sunshine. "I just wish things would have gone differently."

"Don't we all?" Kylee responded. "But you can't live your life dwelling on the if-onlys. Believe me, I'm trying to get past it, too."

"You weren't here," he said, and she flinched.

"Maybe if I was, I would have been with them. I could have been driving the car. Maybe we would have taken another route or been running early. If only I was here, it could have been me with her when she died."

Evan got her point. "I know what you're trying to do. I'm working on it, but I don't know if I'll ever be able to let it go."

Kylee exhaled and picked up a grape, twirling it in her fingers. They watched the children play in silence with only the whisper of scuttling leaves across the grass for sound. "Do you know how I really ended up in New York, Evan?" she asked after a few minutes.

He shook his head.

"Because I couldn't let things go." Kylee said nothing more. Then she got up and wandered over to the playground to help Annabelle get across some monkey bars.

* * *

To Kylee's surprise, Evan arrived a little early at the house on Thursday afternoon, but she didn't mind. She'd told him someone was coming to fix the washing machine, and he'd come early without asking, as if he knew she'd need his help. He took the twins outside while Kylee monitored the repairs on the machine she'd strangled with too much laundry. After being shamed by the mechanic for trying to wash three loads at once, she paid him and coolly hustled him out the door.

When she walked back inside, Evan and the twins were in the kitchen making sandwiches and talking about Christmas trees. He gave her a cocky grin.

"What? I was just trying to be efficient."

"Three loads' worth?"

"Hush," she grumbled, and he laughed. She strolled to the counter, and her stomach growled at the sight of peanut butter and jelly. She reached for the loaf of bread.

"I thought you said you gave this up when you were little."

"Peer pressure." She shrugged and joined them at the table where they talked about the last episode of *Cicero*, then the twins asked about putting up a Christmas tree. "In a few days," Kylee promised, giving Evan a look of dread.

He laughed and informed her they meant their usual fake tree, which was in the shed out back. Then he asked the twins what they wanted for Christmas. Evan thought it would be a good idea to donate some of their old toys to charity, and after much cajoling, Annabelle finally gave in.

"That was a brilliant idea," Kylee murmured as they closed the bedroom door on the children for rest time. Immediately Annabelle's teasing voice echoed behind them, and Kylee rolled her eyes as they headed to the kitchen to clean up.

"Let me help," offered Evan when she insisted she didn't have any other errands to do. They washed dishes together, escorted a few toys to the penalty box for being left out and finally dropped onto the couch. Kylee flipped through the channels on the TV.

"I won't torture you with a documentary," she promised.

Why was she settling in with Evan like they were going to spend the day together? She had things to do to get ready for the move to New York. Not that she minded relaxing with him, but the return to their routine of comfortable friendship after learning about the lawyer had made her feel a little too relieved. A little too happy. She didn't want to be upset with him. She wanted… Her mind scrambled to be realistic and look ahead. She shouldn't enjoy one-on-one time with the twins' godfather, especially since she'd be without him soon.

"So the twins got into the preschool in New York," she blurted.

"I guess that's good news." Evan seemed more disappointed than happy for them.

"It was, but I called in a few favors."

"You're the most persistent woman I know," he murmured.

Kylee wasn't sure if that was a compliment or not. "I just want what's best for them."

"Are you sure moving to New York is what's best for them?" Evan pressed. "The distance? The crowds? Not to mention, taking them away from their grandmother?"

"I know it's not necessarily better, but it's just as good as home," she promised. "And that's where I can best raise them. And remember, we actually have four seasons there. Snow!"

"I'd love for them to see some snow, but there's always vacations. Why not find a good preschool here? We have social media companies in Atlanta, and it's only an hour drive."

She sighed in exasperation. "There's nothing for me locally, though."

"The PTA has a vacancy, I hear."

She groaned. "With an MBA and fifteen years' experience in corporate management managing project teams, do you think running a parent-teacher organization is all I can do?"

"Of course not. I know you can do much more," he said in a rush. "But you would be great in the position. You're a relentless advocate when you want something."

"Thanks, I think," she said. Did that mean he admired her? Or did her persistence bother him? She mentally shrugged.

"Were you always such a go-getter? Mia told me about the time she didn't make the volleyball team, and you went in with her and convinced the coach she could be an alternate in case one of the others backed out."

"And someone did," Kylee pointed out. "Who doesn't have a backup plan?"

He gave her a faint smile. "I guess I don't. Look at what's happened since Chip died. I was all about my job and hanging out with friends until…" He stopped, and she saw his cheeks flush. He gave a nervous laugh.

"Until what?" she probed.

He glanced at her, then back at the television. After a pause, he said, "I figured I'd settle down eventually, but I never made much effort to date until a couple years ago. That didn't work out so I just—well, it was just me and

Chip and Mia... Wow." He gulped as if in sudden horror and turned back to her. "Was I a third wheel?"

She chuckled. "No way, they loved you," she assured him. "You're loyal, dependable and very kind." She thought about her first few days with Henry and Annabelle. "And patient. You have the patience of Job."

He smiled faintly in appreciation. "Not really. I haven't been very patient with God since... Well, I've just been going through the motions taking the twins to church with your mom. The truth is my heart wasn't in it. But seeing how much they needed you has helped me a little bit. This is hard for me, Kylee, and I don't agree with you taking them off to a big city far away, but I admire you for what you're doing."

"Thank you," she whispered. He admired her? She'd single-handedly broken a washing machine and made tuna casserole taboo in the house. She glanced at him with a small smile. Sitting so close, she noticed faint patches of green within his gray eyes and tried to tamp down the urge to move closer to him and search for more.

He studied her back, and her stomach did a flip-flop. Kylee snapped her attention back to a show about backpacking across Europe.

"Mia admired you, too," he said as if that special something hadn't just happened between them.

She gave a low, sarcastic chuckle. "I doubt that."

"What do you mean? It's true."

Kylee shook her head. She'd said goodbye to Mia. She'd failed her as a sister. But she was ready to move on, to do better and to be there for her sister's children.

Evan was relentless. "She bragged to everyone how you put yourself through school and made it in one of the toughest cities in the world."

Her throat tightened. "Well, I didn't deserve that."

"Why not?"

"I… I didn't know she felt that way about me. She was always so popular, I figured she saw me as someone in the way."

Evan reached for Kylee's arm and gave it a soft squeeze. "I'm sorry she never told you how she felt. Maybe she never had the courage."

"Maybe because it was a competition."

"What?"

Kylee met Evan's stare. "Don't you see? I was jealous of her, like you said. I was five years old when she was born, and all of a sudden my younger sister became the apple of my parents' eyes. Of the family. Of everyone." She waved her hand. "Mia was the beautiful and fair one, sweet and funny and talented."

Evan seemed confused. "And you're not talented?"

"It was always a contest between us," she murmured, ashamed. "She outshone everyone around her—at home, at school and always…me."

"I can't believe that's how you felt."

Kylee let out a loud exhale. "That's the real reason I studied hard and left town to go to college. And why I chose New York City to live in. It was as far away as I could get from Mia and provided the best opportunity for me to shine."

Evan squeezed her arm again. This time he didn't let go. She felt his gaze and met his eyes. It didn't matter what he thought of her. She would be gone soon, the twins along with her.

Kylee caught herself inching closer to him. "I was jealous of my sister, Evan. I never had the chance to set things straight with us or make up for always avoiding her, trying to outdo her. That's why I need to raise the twins."

"You were there for her more than you know."

"Oh sure, I was good at giving advice. Only because it made me feel important. I just need… I guess I need to feel important to somebody." She stopped short, cheeks heating. Had she ever given anyone a chance? Is that why she was still single? She'd spent her whole life trying to be better dressed, better looking and more successful than anyone around her. And it hadn't worked. No one ever spoke about her like they did Mia. And for the first time, Kylee understood why. She'd done it all for the wrong reasons. "I didn't deserve her." Her voice thickened. "But I have the twins now," she managed to say, easing her arm from Evan's warm grip.

His touch had sent energy up her shoulders, rolling into her heart and cascading to her toes. More than that, she trusted him. His awareness and concern for others, cool head and earnest sincerity drew her to him like no one else she'd ever met. And maybe it was his tolerance—and acceptance of her.

"I'm going to raise them like Mia wanted me to do, and I have to do it in New York," she added firmly. The twins needed her, not Evan. And he could never care for her like he did his former friends. And that was why, she told herself, she needed to get back to the city by the end of the year. Because lawyer or not, Evan Hollister made her want to stay.

Chapter Eleven

Evan didn't feel right late Tuesday morning. It wasn't a lack of sleep. It wasn't worry over the twins. And it wasn't the nagging guilt and grief that had clung to him for so many months after Mia and Chip's accident. No, suddenly he didn't feel angry at God anymore. In fact, he'd enjoyed the sermon on Sunday as he sat beside Kylee and the twins even though the paperwork for the twins was finally finished.

And yet, something inside his heart was untethered. It felt like a part of him might blow away if he didn't tie himself down. But with the twins taken care of, all he had was his job. Not even Peppy the cat needed him, except for a head rub on the porch steps on occasion.

Evan helped Mrs. Lightfoot rake leaves, then after assuring her that his weekend had been nice, he ran to Brook's Grocery to pick up a few items. He was unable to resist buying the ingredients for macaroni and cheese—just in case. Kylee had discovered the joy of using a slow cooker and learned the finer details pretty quickly. She could cook a few things easily now. She'd just never bothered to learn.

He drove to the cottage with the groceries late that afternoon, thinking about tonight's Nativity practice. He had to show up because he'd volunteered to help build the set, and there was no reason the twins couldn't participate. He told Kylee about the practice, and she quickly agreed to it when the twins hollered with excitement.

Once in the door, he smelled something spicy and delicious. A quick peek in the slow cooker told him that chili was on the menu. The scent made his mouth water.

"Just don't tell me it's leftover turkey," he joked, and Kylee grinned.

"I won't, and it's not." Kylee looked pretty in a white sweater and burgundy leggings, her dark chocolate-looking hair swinging around her shoulders. "Text me if you need me to pick up the twins later at the church," she offered.

He nodded. "Will do." He wished she would stay with him and the kids for the afternoon, but she needed her alone time, and hadn't he asked for this?

She waved to him as she stepped out, closing the front door behind her.

Evan breathed in more of the delicious aromas of tomato and cumin and went over to the counter to stir the pot. "It's time for books!" he called out to the twins.

"We already got them," squawked Annabelle from the back of the house. Chuckling, he breezed down the hall to the children's room, noting the washing machine was chugging along at a normal rate. Seemed she finally figured out laundry, too. In fact, so much was already done that after reading and dinnertime, there was little to clean up, so he packed the kids into his SUV and drove them to church a few minutes early.

"Are we going to play with toys?" queried Annabelle after he explained he'd be busy building a stable.

"No, you're going to play pretend. You can be a sheep or a cow or even a camel. It's a Nativity scene."

"I'll be Wilbur," Annabelle decided.

"What's a Nativity?" asked Henry.

"It's the story about baby Jesus. Do you remember last year when your mother was Mary and your daddy was Joseph?"

"No," replied Annabelle. "Where's Mommy?"

"She's in heaven, remember?"

"Can I be a spider?" Annabelle pushed away the reminder of her parents' absence.

"I remember," said Henry. "They used a doll and pretended it was a baby."

"That's right."

"It was my doll," said Annabelle. "They better not take my doll again."

"They won't," said Evan. "Someone else will bring one. Just pretend to be animals, okay?"

"Okay. And you're going to build a barn?"

"It's kind of like a barn. That's where Jesus was born and put in a manger under a beautiful star."

"What's a manger?" Annabelle asked.

"It's where they put the animals' food," Evan explained.

"That's gross," interjected Henry.

"I don't want my doll in the manger," screeched Annabelle.

Evan sighed, exasperated at her proclamation. It was a good thing they did the Nativity every year so the children could be taught the true meaning of Christmas.

"Are you going to be Joseph now?" asked Henry.

"No." Evan's heart pinched. He was no Chip. "I'm just going to build the manger."

"You can be Joseph, and I can be Mary," Annabelle told her brother.

Henry grunted. "Aunt Kylee can be Mary."

"No, no," said Evan. "A mommy and a daddy will do that."

"Then I'm just going to be a spider." Annabelle sighed

as they pulled into the Good Shepherd Church parking lot. "But I want a star, too." She unhooked herself from her car seat and was out of the SUV before Evan could even help her and rushed inside the annex behind the chapel.

He followed close behind, heart sagging. It wouldn't quite be the same without Chip and Mia in the Nativity, much less celebrating the holidays in their little cottage.

The church's annex was a large room with a small stage at one end and a kitchen on the other. It smelled like long-forgotten potluck dinners, pine cleaner and old chalk. Monk was already setting out tools when Evan met him at the back of the stage.

It took thirty minutes for Sister Lovell to calm the children down and refresh their memories of the Christmas story. Evan stopped hammering long enough to watch her scan her clipboard. Annabelle and Ava were tickling each other, but at least they stayed seated on the carpeted floor. He braced another two-by-four while Monk found a plywood piece for the back.

"Ella Blankenship?" Sister Lovell looked around the room while children continued to gab.

Monk sat back on his heels. "She caught strep throat a few days ago," he called out to her.

Sister Lovell made a face of horror. "I had her down for Mary since we haven't found a couple this year. All of the parents have declined. So she's the oldest of the bunch, and I know she'd sit still."

"Well, she can't make it this year," said Monk.

"Oh, dear…" Sister Lovell looked around the room at the children of various ages.

"Ava, would you like to be Mary?"

"No," scowled the little girl. She crossed her arms over her chest.

"A wise man?" Sister Lovell pleaded.

"No," she repeated.

Ava didn't seem interested in participating this year, thought Evan. He stepped back and watched the children as Monk began to drill holes for strings of lights.

"Would anyone like to be Mary?" called Sister Lovell in frustration.

"I want to be Charlotte!" cried Annabelle from the floor. She scuttled around the carpet like a crab.

Evan put his hands on his hips. He took a deep breath, then strode across the stage and stepped down beside the group of children. "Mary is the most important person in the Nativity besides Jesus," he said loudly, calling the children to order.

They wiggled their feet and some said *baa* in reply.

He caught Annabelle's attention. "Without Mary, there wouldn't have been a baby Jesus. She grew him in her tummy."

"I want to be Mary then." Annabelle jumped to her feet.

He grinned at her. "You would make a great Mary for tonight, Annabelle. Henry? Why don't you be Joseph?"

"But I wanted to be a camel." Henry held up the costume from the costume box. It looked like a fur hoodie with two humps on the back.

"You can drink water from the manger," said Annabelle in excitement.

Another boy waved his hand. "I want to ride the camel. I'll be the cowboy."

"How about you be a king?" Sister Lovell clapped her hands in dramatic excitement. "That's even better. Henry can be Joseph and hold the lantern. We don't have a Joseph yet." She presented an electric lantern she'd brought to Henry.

His eyes widened, impressed by the glowing light.

"Joseph was Jesus's daddy on Earth," said Evan, dropping down to one knee before Henry. "He helped him grow up big and strong and taught him to be a carpenter and make things. Joseph took care of the family."

"Just like my daddy," said Henry. He pondered this for a moment. "But he's not here now."

"You can be just like him," said Evan. "He was Joseph last year."

"Then I want to do it," Henry decided.

"It's just for tonight."

"No, I want to do it for real," he insisted. Something in his little eyes flickered. "I want to take care of the animals and the family."

"Yes," said Annabelle, agreeing with him. "We'll do it at the real time."

Sister Lovell let out a sigh of relief, but Evan stopped her in her tracks. "You know they won't be here for the Nativity, right?"

"What?" Her eyes rounded. "But they just volunteered."

"Unfortunately they're leaving town before Christmas," he explained.

Monk came down to join them as two shepherds began fighting with their staffs. "I think the twins would be an awesome Joseph and Mary," said Monk.

Evan's heart folded. He'd only meant to convince them to be Joseph and Mary for tonight's practice. "Kylee plans to leave the week before Christmas. I told her about the Nativity and the Christmas party, but she plans for them to be in New York."

"Oh, bother," Sister Lovell exclaimed.

Monk patted Evan on the shoulder. "Maybe she'll change her mind."

"She won't," said Evan. "Trust me."

"Then we'll just use the twins for practice until Ella re-covers," Sister Lovell said.

"*If* she recovers in time and is willing." Monk sighed.

"Okay, children. Gather around." Sister Lovell had everything well under control, so Evan returned to the set on the stage. He picked up a ball of lights and began to un-twist them, glancing up to find Monk watching him.

"Maybe if you talk to Kylee, you can change her mind. It seems wrong to take the kids away right before Christmas. Why not let them have one more holiday here in Lagrasse?"

"I know. We've spoken about it, but she has tickets to some gingerbread house show, and she wants to take them to do all those New York things."

Monk frowned. "She can't do it later?"

"I guess Christmastime is the best time."

"That's a shame."

"She has to get back to her job before the end of the year, too," supplied Evan. "Not to mention, she got them into some exclusive preschool."

"I suppose that's exciting." Monk took one end of the lights, and Evan untangled the other end. "I know you're going to miss them."

Of course he would, thought Evan. Kylee's dark eyes hovered in his mind, and the smell of her sultry perfume filled his head. He would miss all three of them. Truth be told, he wanted her to stay as much as he wanted the twins to stay. He liked Kylee, and he liked her with the twins. When they left, he'd lose a part of himself all over again.

Thursday morning, Kylee found herself examining the slow-cooker cookbook harder than an invoice. Evan had raved about her chili when she came home with Christmas presents tucked discreetly under her arms on Tuesday night so she'd sent him to work with the leftovers. Not long afterward, she'd gotten a text from his friend Chase asking for the chili directions, and she sent him a snapshot of it, dumbfounded at the idea that someone had actually asked her for a recipe.

The twins helped her pull the Christmas tree out of the storage shed behind the house after plowing in headfirst with a broom to scare away any spiders. She dragged the tree inside with oven mitts on and a bandanna tied around her mouth, much to the delight of the children, who danced beside her on the cold yellow grass without their shoes or jackets on.

The temperature had dropped, and although she knew it could warm up again, the sharp air made her miss the city. It had flurried in Manhattan the day before, and the team's group chat had been full of complaints, which made her laugh. She didn't miss it now that she wasn't there and didn't mind not having to wear a heavy sweater.

By late afternoon and a phone call with Mom, she was stirring a potato soup in the slow cooker, impressed with how creamy it was even though she hadn't added the cheese yet. It looked and smelled delicious, and with some bits of bacon and some chives salvaged from the garden, it would taste even better. Mia had penciled in *pinch of dry mustard* in the cookbook, and Kylee had found it in the spice cabinet, surprised that mustard actually came in powder form.

When Evan knocked, Annabelle beat her to the door and hung on the handle until Kylee turned the dead bolt. She opened it with a flourish, and he stepped inside with a bag under his arm, wearing a cheerful smile.

"Something smells delicious," he raved.

"It's just soup," said Kylee. "Again."

"What'd you bring me?" asked Annabelle, staring up at him with her head thrown back.

He leaned down and touched his nose to hers. "Books."

"Yay!" she cheered, then pointed to the box in the corner of the living room. "We got a Christmas tree."

"Did you?" He looked at Kylee in surprise.

"We found it in the shed."

"I'm sorry I didn't think of getting it for you. It's pretty dusty out there."

Annabelle grabbed his attention by raising the oven mitts on her hands. "She wore these because of creatures," she tattled.

Evan laughed, and Kylee shrugged. "You know I'd figure out a way."

"Yes, but spiders," he drawled.

"It's winter," she said. "They're gone. I was more worried about mice."

"Charlotte died, but she had babies," said Annabelle. "And they made a new family."

"That's right." Evan kneeled beside her, and Kylee watched him pull a book out of his backpack. "This book is about a little mouse named Stuart. He has a human mommy and daddy who adopt him, and he goes on all kinds of adventures."

"Like what?"

"You'll have to wait and see. Now go get Henry."

"Henry!" Annabelle bellowed, dashing down the hall. "Rest time is over. We got a mouse!"

Evan stood up with a chuckle, and Kylee winced, then raised a brow at the book selection in his hand. "*Stuart Little?*"

"I don't want them to be afraid of the critters."

"Well, you may or may not be able to get them to calm

down enough to read to them. Rest time didn't work out today. There was too much excitement about the tree."

"I can imagine." He studied the tree's crumpled storage box. "Did you want me to set it up?"

Kylee hesitated. She'd planned to use her alone time for a manicure, then stop by Tam's herb shop and buy some honey, but she didn't want to miss out on trimming the tree. She glanced at her nails. They looked fine. "Well, if you want to."

"I don't want to get in the way," Evan said.

"Oh, no, you wouldn't be in the way. Besides, I'm not quite sure what may be hiding inside the box."

"You mean like Stuart Little?" Evan chuckled.

Her eyes narrowed. "Don't tease me." Her plans to have a fun activity with the twins suddenly dissolved into images of being chased down the hall by rodents. But the kids really wanted to set up the tree tonight. And the soup smelled good. She might as well enjoy it, too. "If you don't mind," she said boldly, "you can put the tree up with the kids, and I'll stay here and out of the way or help you if you need it."

"Are you sure?"

"If you're fine with it."

"Of course," said Evan. "But only if you want to. It would be nice if we all did it together."

"I know, but you don't have much time left with the twins. They did like the Nativity practice, and they want to go again."

"Great." Evan seemed to force a smile at the reminder the twins would not be attending the final show. "I mean…yes, they liked the practice. Why don't you stay? It really takes two to get that old tree up. I had to help Chip every year."

"Then you're properly trained." She waved him down the hall. "You go ahead and enjoy your reading time with them, and I'll check the soup and see if I can find the courage to open the box of decorations."

Evan gave her a warm smile that made her feel all happy inside before he headed down the hall to the twins' bedroom, where they promptly erupted into cheers.

Chuckling, she stirred the soup then returned to the living room and stared at the crumpled cardboard box with her sister's messy writing in orange marker: *Ornaments*.

Just as she went back to the kitchen in search of the oven mitts to protect herself from insects and rodents, a text chimed on her phone. She picked it up absent-mindedly. Her intern had managed to secure tickets to the Great Borough Bake-Off. The twins were going to have a good Christmas after all.

It was too bad Evan would not be with them. Her heart spiraled to the floor despite the tickets. It wouldn't be the same without him there. She'd enjoy seeing the excitement of the children, but sharing the time and event with Evan would mean even more.

Chapter Twelve

Henry and Annabelle were so captivated by *Stuart Little* that Evan ended up reading the first two chapters. Just as he was sliding the bookmark in place, he heard dishes clattering in the kitchen. "Come on," he urged the twins, "it's time for dinner."

"Potatoes, yay!" shouted Annabelle.

The kids skipped down the hall, and Evan followed, noting how much time he had left before he needed to leave for work. He wanted to be with the children as much as he could, especially if they were going to decorate the tree. He hadn't bothered to do anything in his apartment, but by the looks of the bags of decorations Kylee had hauled into the house after her errands, he suspected the Maxwell cottage would soon be awash in Christmas cheer.

The soup was so creamy and comforting, he was beyond impressed. "You've really found your niche," he complimented Kylee.

"Oh, it's easy," she said with a flush. "Just potatoes and a few simple vegetables. Nothing to it, really."

"What?" said Evan, pretending to be aghast. "No goat cheese or prosciutto or olives?"

She scrunched up her face, but it didn't stop a grin. "Sometimes a simple dinner is the best meal, I've learned."

"I'll say." Evan had a second helping. The soup would sit well for the night shift, and he already felt a burst of energy after his relaxing time with the twins.

"Who's ready to decorate the tree?" called Kylee.

Evan scrambled to clear the table of dishes before she could start. She looked at him in surprise. "You go ahead," he offered. "I'll take care of these."

"Thanks," she said, then shifted her attention to the living room, where the children were dancing around the old cardboard box containing the tree. A few minutes later, holiday music echoed from a Bluetooth speaker, and the children began to sing along to "Jingle Bells."

Evan was startled to realize one of the voices wasn't coming from the speaker. Kylee could sing. The sound was crystal clear, with perfect pitch, and smooth as butter. Tenderness bloomed in his chest at her sweet timbre, and he quickly wiped his hands on a dish towel and tiptoed into the room.

Henry and Annabelle were jabbing branches into brackets on a green pole while Kylee patiently helped them find the correct slots.

"You're good at this," he said, impressed.

"It's just a big puzzle." She grinned at him. Flickering electric candles they'd found in Mia's Christmas decoration totes reflected from the mirror over the fireplace mantel. They made her eyes look golden and soft.

He looked away, deciding to focus on the tree-trimming project. "Any critters in the box?"

"No, sir."

"I checked for her," Henry informed him with pride.

Evan smirked at Kylee, but she shrugged. "I told you, I don't do critters, and he was happy to help."

"Good job, Henry. You are a brave boy," Evan said.

"And I'm a brave girl," Annabelle chimed in.

Evan picked her up and held her on his hip. "You are one of the bravest girls I know."

"One of the few to climb the General's Tree," joked Kylee.

Evan laughed, set down Annabelle and dragged the container of ornaments over to the tree. He popped it open tentatively, stopped in surprise, then pretended to look concerned.

Kylee froze. "What is it?"

"Oh, nothing to worry about. You just finish putting up the tree." He could have sworn she paled.

"No, seriously. What is it?"

"I want to see!" Annabelle ran over and jerked the box open. Her father's old coonskin hat fell out along with two ball caps.

Kylee let out a scream that split his ears, and Evan put a hand over his mouth to keep from laughing as he held up the other to calm her down. He was too late. The fur hat went one direction, and Kylee went the other, scrambling like a running back and sprinting away for her life. Annabelle put the hat on her head and began to dance around, but Kylee was already down the hall and inside Mia's room with the door slammed shut.

"What's wrong with her?" asked Henry in concern.

Evan couldn't stop laughing. Soon Henry and Annabelle began to giggle, too. In between gasps for air, he heard Kylee calling and finally managed to make his way down the hall but not without taking the coonskin from Annabelle first. He put a finger to his lips at her protest, and the three of them tiptoed to Mia's bedroom.

Evan put the hat behind his back and rapped on the door. "It's okay. You can come out now."

"Did you get it?" Kylee's voice was shrill through the door.

"I did."

The door cracked open, and she peeked out. "What was that? Are the twins okay?"

"Yes, they are." Evan sighed and tried to stay serious. "Because of me. I caught this!" He whipped the hat out and dangled it in the air, and Kylee shrieked and slammed the door shut again.

Evan and the children burst into hysterics.

"It's just a hat, Aunt Kylee! It's a hat!" sang Annabelle.

The bedroom door whipped back open. "What?" Kylee's forehead was furrowed.

Still gasping for air, Evan waggled the hat, making the tail swing.

She swatted at it. "What is that?"

"Just Chip's coonskin hat. You know, the one he bought at the Gateway Arch gift shop."

"No, I did not know. That's horrific!" she cried, but her cheeks started to pull into a smile. He chuckled again. "Oh! You!" scolded Kylee.

"We tricked you," observed Henry with a grin.

Annabelle continued to sing, "It's just a hat! You're a scaredy-cat!"

"I am not," grumbled Kylee. "I'm a T. rex, remember!"

Annabelle let out a falsetto scream and sprinted back to the living room.

Kylee rushed out the door to catch her but barreled straight into Evan instead. He caught her by the elbow and righted himself by wrapping his other arm around her waist. Kylee's smile hovered on her face a few long seconds, and he leaned in and brushed a warm kiss across her lips. Lightning struck, but she pulled away even though she'd kissed him back.

Clearing his throat, Evan dropped his hands and followed her into the living room as if nothing had happened. As if they'd not just been in each other's arms, staring right into each other's eyes. He tossed his head to shake away what he'd done.

A few awkward minutes later, Kylee completed the top of the tree with the branch she'd dropped, while Annabelle started sifting through the ornaments. She picked out a handprint made of construction paper and held it up in the air. "This is mine," she said solemnly.

Evan took a closer look. A small family picture of Mia, Chip and the twins had been snipped into a circle and glued onto the paper hand. "Is that your favorite ornament?" he asked, trying to tamp down his feelings while soothing any grief the children might experience seeing old pictures of their parents.

"Yes," Annabelle decided.

Henry pulled out a glossy hand-painted reindeer. "Do they have reindeers in the stable with Joseph and Jesus?"

"No, champ," said Evan. "Not that I know of."

The little boy frowned. "Then I don't want a reindeer." He tossed the ornament back in the box and strolled over to the tree to watch Kylee unroll a string of new lights. "What are those?"

"They're lights to make the tree sparkle."

"Like the Christmas star?"

"Yes, like stars." She glanced at Evan.

"The star told the shepherds where to go," said Henry. "And the kings, too. And their camels."

"Wow, you remember your lesson on the Nativity story, Henry," said Kylee, impressed. "We'll put one on the very top after we finish hanging the ornaments to remind us to look up when we're lost."

"Yes!" cheered Annabelle.

"And it will show us where to go." Henry picked the reindeer up off the floor.

Evan looked at Kylee, and she faintly smiled when he caught her eye, but she held his gaze for so long that his heart started thumping again. He knew where he wanted to be, but did she feel the same way? In his heart, he knew she belonged in Lagrasse, and he wanted her to belong with him.

After the tree was finished, Kylee popped some popcorn, knowing it was better than giving the twins anything too sugary. Popcorn was also simple enough to make using the microwave, because her brain was stuck on loop of the kiss Evan had given her. And she'd returned it willingly as if she wasn't leaving soon. It left her happy but confused.

Forcing herself to pretend it hadn't happened, she marched the popcorn bowl into the living room. By the time the snack was devoured and *Rudolph the Red-Nosed Reindeer* read in Evan's best voice, the children were hustled off to bed. Kylee suggested that Evan tuck them in, knowing their time together was drawing near to an end. More than likely, this would be his last Christmas season with them.

He would miss the children terribly, she thought with regret, as she cleaned the popcorn bowl and put it away. So would she. She couldn't be selfish, especially not at Christmas. He should spend as much time as he wanted with them while they were still in Lagrasse, she decided. And she didn't mind. They loved him, and she... Well, it was too bad that he and she were so different. Kylee dug around in the pantry for the broom. They had different ideas about what was best for the children, too. The kiss had been agreeable, too agreeable. Better to forget it.

With a sigh, Kylee checked the clock on the stove and

padded into the living room with its glowing, soft white lights. The tree made everything feel cozy and relaxing. She sat on the couch, exhausted but content. Popcorn and potato soup, giggles and homemade Christmas ornaments. She could hardly wait to try making gingerbread houses. Oh, the joy of putting one's own gingerbread walls together with frosting and a bounty of candy to decorate, or eat when no one was looking. Memories of building gingerbread houses with Mia came flooding back to her.

Evan tiptoed into the living room from the hallway. She watched him appraise the tree.

"Does it pass inspection?" Kylee teased.

"It may be several years old, but none of the wiring is bent or chewed. It passes."

"And the lights are brand-new."

"Yes. It was smart of you to do that. I do think I'll miss seeing lights on the roof this year, though." He glanced out the front window.

"Mia and Chip did that?" Lights on the roofline of the little cottage would be lovely. She sighed. "I think they'd be happy with the tree."

"I think they'd be happy about a lot of things." Evan eased down beside her on the sofa, and Kylee's heart flickered. He smelled like soap and pine. She wanted to cuddle up beside his muscled arms and rest her head on his shoulder. Another kiss was a tempting idea. Instead, she trained her eyes on the tree. Her reaction was silly. Ridiculous. Schoolgirl stuff. But the butterflies in her stomach danced.

"You're doing a great job with the kids," he said, oblivious to her thoughts. He exhaled. "I owe you an apology."

"No, you don't," she replied.

"Actually, I do. I wasn't any different. I was trying to

do everything by myself, too—keep an eye on your mom, watch the twins, take care of the house, do my job…"

Kylee realized how much Mia had had on her plate and was suddenly grateful for Chip. "I've told you before, you don't have to apologize for what happened, Evan. No one blames you, so stop blaming yourself."

He looked over at her, eyes glowing in lighting that shouldn't have been so romantic. She resisted the urge to reach up and cup his jaw, and a shiver zigzagged down her spine in protest. They stared at one another for several long seconds.

"I should have known Mia would not have trusted her children around anyone less than worthy," she said at last. "You're a good person, Evan."

"And the same goes for you." He held out a hand, and she took it, but instead of shaking it, he wrapped his fingers around hers. "I hope you don't mind a few visits now and then," he warned. "I've always wanted to see New York."

Kylee sat up, surprised at how her heart soared at his touch—and the idea. Her mind began to spin with possibilities, plans. She pushed them away. "I'm sorry about the kiss. We shouldn't have."

"No?" Evan interrupted.

She shook her head. "No, we just got carried away. Right?"

Evan pulled his hand from hers. "Right." He exhaled. "Look, I was wondering if you'd put off taking the kids up to New York for just one more week."

"That would mean leaving after Christmas," she said, heaviness plopping onto her heart like a paperweight.

"Yes, I know," Evan admitted. "The thing is, Henry and Annabelle played Mary and Joseph at Nativity practice."

Kylee furrowed her brow. "Why?"

He sighed. "I told them the children would be gone by Christmas, but they did so well and were so cute. Kylee…" Evan turned sideways and curled a leg up onto the couch. "Annabelle took the role very seriously, and Henry, he was really sweet. He remembers his dad doing it last year. He *remembers*," emphasized Evan.

The inflection stabbed her chest. Of course she didn't want the twins to forget their time with their father. "I'm sorry, Evan, but I already have the plane tickets, and there's the gingerbread house show."

"Oh."

Kylee was filled with disappointment when she could have sworn he inched away.

"They'll love it," she insisted, reminding herself she shouldn't be kissing or hand-holding with the twins' god-father. "Annabelle will be thrilled. Mia always wanted to go, and I did, too. I'd always planned—" Her throat caught. "I'd planned to take Mia someday. The twins will love it," she reasserted. "They'll have the best time. I'm sorry, Evan. We can't stay for Christmas." A small voice in the back of Kylee's mind suggested she invite Evan, too, but he was going to care for the cottage until she decided what to do with it, and he had his shifts at the firehouse.

The room fell into an uncomfortable silence. Kylee was sure he could hear her heart pounding, and for all the wrong reasons.

Evan got up suddenly from the couch. "Well, I guess that's that then. I hope you don't mind if I keep taking them to the practices until you leave, though."

"I don't."

Evan stood there awkwardly for a moment, then announced, "I better get to work."

"Did you want to take the leftover soup?"

"Yes, but I—no. You keep it. Annabelle loved it, and I'm sure she'd be happy to have it for lunch tomorrow."

Kylee felt like something was wrong. If only he understood how important it was to give the twins a Christmas they wouldn't forget so they didn't dwell on their parents too much. He didn't seem to appreciate all she was offering them. "Okay," she said, regrets piling up like neglected files.

She got up and walked him to the door, and when she locked it behind him, her knees felt weak. It was a feeling that frightened her, more than a kiss, because she knew when she left town she'd never feel it again. Her heart wouldn't jump when he walked into a room. Her shoulders wouldn't relax at his soft, comforting voice. She wouldn't have his advice, his listening ear or even be able to see his wacky sense of humor when he interacted with the children every day.

Kylee braced her heart. She needed to remember how important the holidays were for the children, too. Evan really loved the twins, she realized. Truly. She felt her throat tighten. How she felt about him couldn't matter. She'd be fine without him in New York. She'd always been able to work things out on her own.

Kylee began packing things for the twins to take to their new home. Evan would see that the lawn was mowed. The house could be rented out and the money stashed away for maintenance and the twins' futures. Mia's room was sufficiently decluttered, and the kitchen was organized and cleaned out except for the cookbooks. Those Kylee would ship to New York. They were a part of her sister that she could hold on to forever.

Packing up the twins' things kept her mind off the momentous task of raising them while balancing a demanding career. She tried not to think about working less overtime or how she would handle drop-off and pick them up at school each day. She certainly wouldn't be the first one in the office anymore, and she wouldn't be the last to leave, but she couldn't imagine not making sure the kids saw her face each morning and evening. She didn't want them to feel alone.

She knew what that was like. She'd make sure they knew they were loved. And she'd make certain Evan never had a reason to think she couldn't get the job done.

Kylee cared what he thought, she realized, and she cared about him. A lot. Wouldn't her little sister be delighted that they'd become friendly? A whisper of regret tugged at her heart, but she refused to let it bother her. With two little people added to her already busy life, she certainly didn't need to wish for anything else—especially with someone who thought Lagrasse was the center of the universe. If she ever settled down and got married, it would be with someone who cared more about her than himself, loved the children and could cook... But Evan wasn't for her. He'd be wonderful for someone someday. Just not her.

On Tuesday, Kylee wrapped presents in Mia's room while the twins giggled during rest time, waiting impatiently for Evan to arrive so he could continue *Stuart Little*. Dinner was already warming in the slow cooker—a simple but elegant minestrone. She'd asked Evan to pick up a baguette at The Last Re-Torte to go with the soup.

When he knocked on the door, her heart flip-flopped with anticipation. She was getting too used to this—the cottage, the homemaking and the man who dropped by almost every day. Her life was in New York, not here in Lagrasse.

"Come in," she called, and heard Evan's key jiggle in the

lock at her invitation. He burst in, shaking himself dry from a light sprinkling of rain that left glistening spots in his hair. His dark blue uniform shirt was speckled with water. He held up a bag. "I bought the bread." He grinned. "And I didn't take one bite out of it on the way here."

"That was very thoughtful of you," she joked. Taking the bag from him, she swung her gaze away when their eyes met. She shouldn't be so happy to see him after the way he left Tuesday, when he'd asked her to let the twins stay in town until Christmas, but she was. She shouldn't look forward to having dinner with him, but she did. And most concerning of all, she shouldn't be hoping he would stay a few minutes after the children went to bed so they could talk. "Did you manage to get some sleep?" she asked him.

"I did. How's the packing going?"

"All right."

"And you're sure you don't mind if I take the children to the Nativity practice tomorrow? The annex was already reserved for tonight."

She shook her head. "As long as they understand they won't be there for the final performance."

Evan bobbed his chin in a sharp nod. "I'll make sure."

Kylee didn't miss the disappearance of his smile as he looked away. "It's just a Nativity," she said as she put the bread on the counter. "I can find one for them to see in New York."

He leaned against the kitchen wall with his hands in his pockets. "The Nativity is our tradition. Chip and I worked on the sets together and included the kids when they came along. When Henry was an infant, they used him as a real baby Jesus."

"That's so sweet," Kylee said. Then she took a deep breath. "I think it's best that we leave before Christmas. I know moving in the middle of a holiday will be distracting, but I think it'll keep their mind off of the fact that their parents aren't here."

"Would it be such a bad thing, for them to remember?" Evan looked quizzical.

Trying not to look at his firm arms folded across his chest, she turned to dig around in the sink for a dish to rinse. "I don't want them to be sad."

Evan remained silent as if he disagreed, or maybe he'd surrendered to the idea.

Kylee dropped her hands to her sides. "Evan, you do not have to do penance by seeing these kids every day and worrying about every little thing."

"They've been a part of my life since they were born. It's hard to think about life without them," he admitted.

"You can call them whenever you like. Maybe read to them every night via video chat," Kylee suggested.

His face lit up. "That's a great idea!" He surprised her by throwing his arms around her waist and lifting her into the air. Then as if realizing what he'd done, he froze, and she slid down until her feet touched the floor, and they stood face-to-face.

The feeling of his heart beating against hers seemed to turn her legs into jelly. She couldn't think, she couldn't make herself pull away. It was breathtaking, electric and peaceful all at the same time.

Evan moved first, and Kylee broke contact, unable to look him in the eye, swiveling her attention back to the pots and pans in the sink. She cleared her throat. "Yes, that's fine. I mean, it would comfort them and help them get adjusted to the change."

"Right," he agreed, his soft tone daring her to look at him and address what just occurred.

"Uncle Evan! Are you here yet?" Annabelle called from down the hall.

Evan remained still. Kylee could feel his gaze on her and wondered what he was thinking. She kept her eyes on the dishes in the sink.

"Guess I'll go read to the kids now," he said. "Thanks for letting me take them to practice tomorrow."

"Sure."

"You can come along if you want."

She finally turned and met his stare. "No, thanks. I still have a lot of packing to do. And video meetings for work."

"Suit yourself."

He walked away, and Kylee's eyes burned with unshed tears. She hated that Evan would miss Christmas with the twins. She hated that she would miss him, too. She took a deep breath and exhaled. But she had to make memories with her sister's children, who were now her responsibility.

Chapter Thirteen

Evan tried to focus while he read the next chapter of the new book to the twins. Henry lay beside him on the floor, with Annabelle on the top bunk behind them, hanging over the edge like a limp noodle.

Evan's pulse pounded as if he'd touched a live wire. Embracing Kylee had been unplanned. The sensation of being so close to her in that way made him want to hold her again. Kiss her.

Be cool, he thought to himself. He had the twins to consider. Besides helping them get packed and to the airport in a week, he had no real reason to spend any extra time with their aunt. Yet whenever he lingered and they talked, laughed or even cried together, everything else in his life seemed to take a back seat.

The beckoning smell of dinner broke his concentration. When had he ever enjoyed soup so much? He put down the book.

"Aw," complained Henry, still riveted by Stuart's adventures.

"It'll be time to eat soon. Do you want to play outside?"

"We already did," said Henry. "It was too cold."

"Let's play dinosaurs," shouted Annabelle from overhead.

Evan grinned up at her. "You get started. Find us some good leaves on the tallest tree to eat," he suggested.

His phone buzzed, and he saw a message from James about this morning's interview for the lieutenant position. Smile fading, he slid the phone back into his pocket.

Henry opened the toy box and began to dig around.

"Don't pull out too many," Evan admonished him before stepping into the hall. He heard the television; Kylee must be watching the news as she folded laundry, blissfully unaware that he would trade the promotion for a chance to talk her into staying in Lagrasse.

He went to the back door and looked out the window. It was nearly dark, the winter sky highlighting a waning moon over the bare trees. He studied the hammocks in the backyard, realizing he should have brought them in by now. There were no toys left outside except a half-inflated basketball still too big for Henry's and Annabelle's little hands. Maybe they'd play someday. Chip would have loved that.

Evan checked his watch. He shouldn't stay long tonight if Kylee stayed in. And he hoped she did...

Thump.

The crash from the twins' bedroom rattled the house.

"What in the world?" exclaimed Kylee, darting in from the family room. She had a jacket on, which meant she hadn't planned to eat with them after all. Evan rushed with her to the bedroom, brushing past her when she froze at the door.

Annabelle was lying spread-eagled on the floor, looking at the ceiling, her lips slack. Henry stared at her from where he sat cross-legged on the floor. He looked surprised, eyes wide, mouth trying to say something.

"Henry, what happened?" Evan dropped to his knees.

Annabelle suddenly curled into a ball and clutched her head.

"Annabelle!" cried Kylee.

Evan felt her rush up behind him to scoop up the little girl, but he barred her with an arm. "Wait." Evan laid a gentle hand on the child's cheek. "Annabelle?" he whispered.

She rolled to her side and released a strangled sob.

"What happened, Henry?" Kylee repeated, but Evan said, "Let's stay calm. It's not Henry's fault, clearly."

"She was on the top bunk," cried the little boy, eyes tearing up. "She growled at me and then she fell down."

"From the top?" Kylee gasped.

The fear in her tone made Evan want to embrace her again. "It's going to be fine."

"She doesn't look fine!"

"If she's crying, she's breathing," Evan reminded her.

Henry began to cry, too, and Kylee hurried over and picked him up and held him. "It's okay, baby," she said, rocking him back and forth, but her eyes were on his sister.

Evan glanced at the top bunk. It was high, but the floor was carpeted with a thick shag rug.

Annabelle continued to sob.

"Are you okay?" he whispered. He slid his hands down her arms and then her legs. Leaking giant tears, she crooked her head up at him. "Does it hurt to look at me?" he asked.

"N-no."

Evan gently examined her neck, and she didn't flinch. "Where does it hurt?"

Annabelle pointed at the crown of her head, and he touched it lightly. She didn't respond. He picked her up carefully and held her. "You're going to be okay. You just took a spill." He rubbed her head, and she swatted at him.

"Ow!"

Kylee chuckled from behind him. "There she is. I'd say she's okay."

Evan tried not to laugh and further irritate the little girl. "Let's go sit on the couch and rest awhile."

"Why?" grumbled Annabelle, still cross.

"Because you have a very high threshold of pain, and I want to make sure you're okay. You could have broken your arm."

"It's not broken," Annabelle grunted.

"Well, dinner's ready if you're hungry," suggested Kylee.

"Okay." Annabelle sighed as Evan wiped her tears.

Henry said, "I'm hungry."

"Come on then," Kylee insisted. "Let's go get you some dinner."

"Didn't you have your errands?" Evan asked. "Why don't you go ahead, and I'll make their dinner?"

"No, I can't. I should stay."

"I'm sure she's okay, and I'll call you if anything changes. Promise."

"If you're sure." Kylee hesitated. "I do have some shopping to do for the trip."

The reality that the twins were leaving in a week crashed back down on him. "Of course." He needed to spend more time with them, and Kylee wasn't a part of that.

"I'll be back in a bit." She nodded toward Annabelle. "I've seen her drop out of the hammock a hundred times. She's tough."

"Right. We'll be okay." Evan waited until Kylee grabbed her handbag and gave her a wave. "I'll watch her closely," he promised, hoping it would be the distraction he needed.

Although she enjoyed having a few hours to herself, Kylee was glad to get back home and make sure Annabelle was all right. The truth was, being on leave from work meant less stress, less hurry, less worry… No. There was worry, and stress, too, just of a different kind. These sacrifices weren't to impress anyone or to receive a big paycheck. They were for Mia. For the twins. And, Kylee realized, for herself.

She wanted to be here. She wanted to be a mother. Even if she wasn't as good at it as her mom or her sister. Even if she had a different way of doing things. And even if Evan teased her a little.

The thought of the twins' godfather filled her with a happy warmth. Sometimes he looked at her like he cared about her. He'd even kissed her. Her stomach filled with butterflies at the memory of their embrace at the kitchen sink. He was too honorable to pretend he hadn't meant it. She'd seen it in his eyes, and she'd felt it, too.

It didn't seem like life was one endless, repetitive cycle anymore. It felt like someone had hit a reset button, and she was in a familiar but new world. A place where she was needed. A beautiful place with beautiful people she'd been so busy trying to outshine that she hadn't taken the time to notice them. Being in the spotlight didn't make anyone more loved and appreciated than when they were working in the wings. And that suited her for now.

So did Evan, if she was honest.

The news on the television hummed in the background, and the tree twinkled—dancing lights that reminded her of laughter and joy. She loved it. Not just the peace, but the sense of belonging, of truly being home.

Kylee smiled to herself as she studied Annabelle sitting beside her. She'd kept her up a little longer than usual, but the little girl leaning on her arm was dozing now. Kylee picked her up and carried her down the hall toward the bedroom where Henry was already asleep. Holding the little girl to her chest, Kylee smelled baby shampoo that reminded her of when Annabelle was an infant.

Just as Kylee reached the bedroom door, Annabelle raised herself off of Kylee's shoulder with a sudden choking cough. The little girl's face wrinkled. "I'm… I'm…"

"You're okay," Kylee whispered. "I'm taking you to bed."

"I want my momma." The little girl began to cry. "What happened?"

Something snapped in Kylee's chest. "Annabelle, it's okay. I'm here." Tensing, she patted her on the back.

The little girl's neck wobbled. "My head hurts," she whined.

Kylee reached for the hall light switch. When it blinked on, Annabelle squeezed her eyes shut. She was pale, dazed. "It's okay, honey," said Kylee. "We can get you some medicine." She'd seen a bottle of children's acetaminophen in the medicine cabinet.

Annabelle howled, "I want my—" Then she stopped, eyes widening, and slumped back over Kylee's shoulder only to get sick.

Kylee had a moment of shock before panic set in. She rushed the little girl to the bathroom, snatching at towels, and laid her on the bath rug. "Annabelle! Annabelle! Are you okay?"

The little girl stared woozily up at the ceiling.

"Annabelle?" Something was wrong. Kylee realized her lungs were sucking air like she was speeding down a bumpy road. She'd promised to keep these children safe and happy. They were her family. Her babies.

Tears poured from her eyes as she ran for her phone.

Evan jumped from the couch in the firehouse's day room and cheered after the Atlanta Hawks made another basket.

The lieutenant job interview earlier that morning had been brief but positive. He grinned at Chase across the room, euphoric.

"We're going to take this one," his partner cried.

The other paramedics and firefighters rumbled in agreement as they munched on trays of frosted sugar cookies that a family had dropped off as a gift. They were as good as The Last Re-Torte Bakery's, and the lopsided homemade icing and strange choice of colors were adorable.

It couldn't have been a better couple days, Evan decided. He'd seen the twins and survived the interview for the promotion that James had insisted he try for. Returning to the TV, Evan's eyes glazed over, thinking back to earlier in the day. His good mood wasn't all because of the children. It was Kylee. He was drawn to her like a mariner to the stars. He loved her company. He thought she was beautiful. The most casual touch filled him with happiness.

The thought startled him as the room echoed with excitement again, and he joined in but only half-heartedly. His true joy was back at the cottage.

"Hey! Hollister!" called Shawna from across the room. She picked up Evan's phone from the end table next to her and waved it. "Your phone has rung twice."

"Thanks, I didn't hear it." Evan grinned. Shawna tossed it across the room, and he caught it, eyeing the time stamp in surprise. Was it so late already? It seemed like he'd just clocked in, but it was only an hour from midnight. What a blessing, he thought, to have such a quiet shift. No fires, no health scares, no family dramas. It was almost perfect and, except for the basketball game, a silent night. His smile faded. But *the* silent night was a week away on the holiest night of the year. And the twins wouldn't be here. Neither would Kylee. They'd be in New York.

Evan's cheer evaporated as he leaned back beside James, who was riveted to the game. He pulled up his missed calls. To his surprise, they were all from Kylee. Then the phone chirped, and her name popped up on the screen again. Call number three in under four minutes.

Evan jumped up from the couch and put the cell phone to his ear, striding to the kitchen so he could hear. "Hello?"

"Evan? Are you there?" Her throaty voice came out in tight gasps.

He froze at the door. "Yes. What's wrong?"

"It's Annabelle. She's... She got sick. She said her head hurts, and she's acting weird and staring into space. She even asked me what happened. She doesn't have a fever..." Kylee's voice pitched high. "I don't know what to do!"

Those were words he never thought he'd hear from her, and they filled Evan with alarm. "Stay put," he spluttered. He took a deep breath. He ordered his brain to collect itself. He was standing in the middle of a fire station. Wearing a uniform. "Stay with her. I'll be there in a minute."

Evan dashed out of the kitchen, hit the alarm on the wall, and everyone jumped to their feet. "My niece!" he cried as he ran for his truck.

Chase was on his heels at once. Their medic bags were already packed inside their vehicle for the shift, and Chase hit the sirens as Evan peeled out of the garage. He had to force himself not to speed recklessly through town as he raced for the cottage.

When he reached it, the front porch light flicked on, and the door slammed open. He saw the back of Kylee's head as she dashed back into the house, and a thousand thoughts whirled in his head: symptoms, diagnoses, responses, outcomes. And then the memories intruded: Chip. Mia. The funeral.

Evan's heart thundered in his chest so hard he had to remember to breathe with each stride into the house. The bathroom light was on, and he rounded the corner to find Kylee on her hands and knees, looking over Annabelle on the bathroom floor.

The girl was unresponsive. There were towels on the rug, and the room smelled sour and damp.

Evan struggled to push overwhelming anxiety to the back of his consciousness and let his paramedic training kick in. "Move over," he said, forcing himself to sound confident and in control.

Kylee sat back, tears in her enormous brown eyes. Her normally olive complexion looked as white as a sheet.

Evan felt Chase come in behind him. They checked the little girl's breathing and pulse, then Evan whipped out his penlight with the pupil gauge and studied her eyes. They were dilated. Her head, he remembered. She'd fallen from the bunk. How had he missed it? Why didn't he think to check?

"Concussion," he murmured to Chase. Her symptoms had been delayed.

The distant wail of an ambulance filled his ears, signaling more help had come, and Kylee jumped up and ran out of the room.

It was all Evan could do not to scoop the child into his arms and hold her as if he could heal her with his love. But he could not. It was up to God, he realized.

Another paramedic arrived with a gurney, and Annabelle was transferred onto it wearing a cervical collar to stabilize her neck. Evan grabbed one end of the gurney and guided it out into the hall, fighting the urge to order everyone to hurry.

Kylee was standing in the twins' bedroom door holding Henry on her hip. Both of their faces were as frozen as marble.

Evan tried to give them a reassuring smile, but his face felt too heavy. "County hospital," he rasped to Kylee, then turned his attention back to the little girl who'd been left in his care.

Kylee followed the ambulance to the hospital with her heart throbbing all the way. Annabelle had gone immediately for a CT scan, and Evan paced in the hall while Kylee sat in a hard chair in the waiting room with Henry, praying. To her relief, her mother soon arrived and took Henry home after they were assured Annabelle was stable. As soon as they left, Kylee dashed to the front desk and pleaded to be allowed back to the treatment rooms where her niece was being examined.

She took a seat in the quiet sterile room next to the little girl curled up in a warming blanket and held her hand. Where Evan had disappeared to now, she didn't know.

The child whimpered in her half sleep. Kylee felt so nauseous she could barely sit up straight, and her throat ached from the tension. A small heart rate monitor on the tip of Annabelle's finger made a blip on a screen, and Kylee listened to the tune of the little girl's pulse. Guilt snowballed in her brain. What had she been thinking, allowing Annabelle to play on the top bunk? Why had she taken the chance, especially knowing how active the children were?

Her mouth parched, Kylee swallowed and studied a dry-erase board with the date scribbled across the top. Six more days until they were to leave for New York. But would it be safe for Annabelle to fly? How long did recovery take? What if she didn't recover at all? Kylee's head ached, and she massaged her temples. If she didn't get back to work soon, she would really be out of the loop, behind, but if she did… Images of the children swirled in her mind. Evan was there, too.

A doctor with white streaks in his cropped silver hair appeared at the door to Annabelle's room. He smiled at her, but it gave little comfort. "You look distraught."

"I am."

"It's a mild concussion," he said. "She's going to be okay. There's not any bleeding and very little swelling. She's just disoriented."

Relief washed over Kylee. "It could have been so much worse," she began. "My sister… She's…not here."

The doctor smiled at her again. "I'm sorry. You're doing a good thing for Annabelle. Count your blessings that it's not more serious. Children this age can get into all kinds of trouble if they're not watched closely. They don't always think about the consequences."

Kylee nodded. She hadn't been watching them. She'd been in the other room thinking about Evan, her career, getting back to Manhattan. She'd been thinking about herself. As always. This was her fault.

The doctor offered her a pamphlet about head injuries, and she accepted it with shaky hands. "Did you mean you have custody?" he asked.

Kylee nodded.

"So you're her mother now," he assumed.

"I'm just the aunt," she said.

He glanced at his clipboard, then turned to leave, promising to talk to her later.

Being an aunt didn't make her a mother. She couldn't keep a goldfish alive. She destroyed washing machines. She burned egg noodles and could only use a slow cooker. She didn't belong in Lagrasse.

"I don't fit in here," she whispered. She reached out and rested a hand on Annabelle's arm. The little girl was alert now, staring dully at the wall, unable to sleep because of what they'd given her to stay awake. "I don't belong here," said Kylee a little louder. "With you. With Henry."

As if in agreement, Annabelle turned to look at her with pleading eyes. "Where's Evan?" she sobbed. "I want to go home."

"He's in the hall," said Kylee, overcome by an avalanche of relief. Annabelle wanted Evan. Needed him. Because he was best. He'd been right from the beginning. The twins belonged with him. She was the intruder. "I'll get him," she whispered.

Kylee eased out of her chair and, once outside the room, rushed down the hall looking wildly for him.

He appeared through a double set of doors as though he'd heard her inner cries. "Is she okay?" he called, his calm composure changing to alarm.

Kylee reached for his hands when they met, but he wrapped her in a warm, tight hug. "She's okay." Kylee didn't want to break away, to lose the way they fit together, but she had to do it. She forced herself to step back out of his tenderness and beckoned him. "Come on. She wants to see you." Kylee knew she sounded helpless, but there was nothing else she could do for Annabelle, except...home. She wanted to go home.

Evan followed Kylee to the room where the monitor was still chirping at regular intervals. He hurried to the bed. "Annabelle," he whispered. The little girl moved slightly, and he draped an arm over her and laid his head beside hers. "You're going to be okay. The doctors said you're going to be just fine."

"What happened?"

"You bumped your head."

"Where's Henry?"

"He's with Nanna," Evan replied.

"I want to go back to my house."

"I know you do, honey. Aunt Kylee will take you home in a few hours. You rest now."

Annabelle quieted.

Evan straightened and turned to Kylee where she was leaning against the wall. She realized she was chewing on a fingernail. Her chest hurt from fighting tears. He walked over and searched her face, eyes glossy as if he wanted to cry, too.

"It's all my fault," Kylee blurted.

He looked startled. "What do you mean? It's mine."

"No."

"Yes, it is." His eyes started to drip at the corners, whisking the breath out of Kylee's lungs. "I should have known to check for a concussion. This is my fault, Kylee. I should have watched for the symptoms." He swiped at his cheek with the back of his wrist. "I don't belong in this uniform. I don't deserve guardianship of the twins. Mia made the right call giving you custody."

What? Evan Hollister was hurting and crying because of her? "I'm going back to New York," Kylee announced.

"I know, but—"

Kylee shook her head. "You are a better guardian than I could ever be." A tear escaped, and she smiled without feeling. "Mia wasn't right about this."

"But, Kylee, I..." Evan looked confused.

"It was an accident. And it was my fault, not yours," Kylee insisted.

"Honey, you are the best thing that could have happened to them. I am not the answer here."

"No." Kylee shook her head. Suddenly, she felt a switch flip, and her legs started moving of their own accord. "I'm leaving. You stay with Annabelle."

"Kylee!" exclaimed Evan.

She shook her head vehemently. "I can't do it, Evan. You love them, and they love you. I'm the problem in this equation." She forced herself to hurry from the room before he said anything more.

Chapter Fourteen

The air was crisp and cool the next day with late afternoon clouds hurrying across the horizon as if they were on a mission. The beautiful Christmas decorations on the Lightfoots' house should have brought Evan some comfort, but they didn't. He slammed the door to his SUV and pounded up the stairs to his apartment. Peppy didn't meet him, and he was surprised it bothered him.

He paced the small apartment, his body heavy and mind feeling like sludge. Kylee had been in fight-or-flight mode at the hospital. It seemed she would do anything to escape the guilt she felt, but she didn't deserve it.

Evan tumbled onto the couch and clutched his head. What kind of paramedic didn't think to check for a concussion? It could have been more serious, and to make matters worse, Kylee blamed herself when he was the one who had let everyone down. This was all on him. He had no business wearing a paramedic uniform. If he really wanted to do the right thing by his friends, he would turn in his badge and do something else. Maybe he could try raising vegetables or working part-time at Brook's Grocery.

Mia *had* made the right decision choosing Kylee to be Henry and Annabelle's guardian. He had no right raising the twins. He didn't know what was best for them, and he obviously couldn't keep them safe. They would be adored and spoiled in New York. He could let them go now. He had to.

Just then, his phone chirped.

"Evan?" James's familiar voice filled his head, friendly and soothing. "How is Annabelle?"

"She's going to be okay, most likely," replied Evan.

"Most likely?"

"It was a concussion."

"Did they admit her?"

"No," relented Evan. "Mrs. Spokes came back with Henry, and they took her home a few hours ago."

"Then I'm sure she'll be fine."

"I guess."

"Hey, if she wasn't admitted, she's fine. It could have been much worse."

"I know, and that's on me."

"Come on, Evan. Anyone could have missed it, especially since she didn't have symptoms at first."

Evan refused to accept that. "I'm her godfather and a paramedic. I didn't do my job." *Again.*

"You handled everything professionally as soon as you were informed. Don't beat yourself up. We need you at your best."

Evan stiffened. "What's wrong?" Was there another disaster in Lagrasse today? He wasn't sure he was up for it.

"It's nothing serious," James assured him. "Unless you count being promoted."

Evan clutched the phone tighter and blinked. "What?"

"It came down the pipeline a few minutes ago. I thought I'd call. Congratulations, Lieutenant Hollister."

"Lieutenant," repeated Evan as much to himself as to James.

"That's right. You've earned it, man. Congratulations."

What should have been a compliment felt like a cold steel barb. Evan shook his head. "No, I can't accept it."

"What do you mean, you can't accept it?" James's tone held disbelief.

"Look what just happened to Annabelle," Evan pointed out. He didn't bother to mention Mia and Chip again. "No, James, I can't do it."

"Yes, you can," insisted his mentor.

"No." Evan resisted the urge to feel any excitement. "I'm not cut out for this career, Captain. It may have been an ambition of mine once, but I'm going to have to change course."

"Don't be ridiculous. You've dreamed about doing this all your life."

"Then I need a new dream. One that doesn't end up with other people hurt."

There was a heavy silence on the other end of the line.

Evan exhaled. "I should get some sleep. I told Mrs. Spokes I'd drop by the cottage and check on things."

"Good of you," mumbled James. "What do you want me to tell the brass?"

"That I can't accept the promotion."

"Evan? Are you sure? You know I'm looking at retirement soon. Maybe you should think it over a few days. Talk with your family and friends. I'm not going to tell them anything yet."

Evan sighed with fatigue and frustration. "Sure, Captain." But he knew he wouldn't change his mind.

How could he?

Exhaustion had been her constant companion the past two days, and as soon as Mom came over to the house on Friday, Kylee tiptoed into the twins' bedroom and lay down to rest beside Annabelle, who'd fallen asleep. She'd quickly returned to her usual self yesterday, except for being eager for rest time. Today, Henry had pleaded to stay up, and Kylee had given him an extra thirty minutes to sit with his grandma. He would lie down on the couch, he promised, and stare at the Christmas tree star.

Kylee studied Annabelle sleeping beside her. Her bangs were pushed at an angle across her forehead, the ends nearly to her lashes. She needed a haircut. Kylee wondered why she hadn't noticed. Had she been so busy planning their exodus to New York City, she'd dropped the ball on their care?

She stared at the top bunk overhead. She hadn't used any common sense when it came to the twins' safety. It was a mistake, she thought to herself, for Mia to purchase such a bed while they were so young, but no doubt her sister had only been thinking ahead and trying to get the most for her money. That was something Kylee didn't worry about very often anymore, but there was no pride in the admission. She'd missed out on plenty of things that were more important. Her eyes blurred. And she'd have to do it again.

Kylee pressed her arm against Annabelle's little body to feel her radiating warmth. Evan's instincts had been right. She should never have accepted custody. He'd been smart to get a lawyer, and a gentleman to let things go, but it'd been a mistake. He was the right person for the job. The wonderful, godly man was proof that family wasn't about blood but devotion and ability. If he hadn't come so quickly, she may have waited longer and tried to figure things out on her own. Kylee's heart recoiled when she admitted that Annabelle could have died, and it would have been her fault.

Knowing Mom would be devastated when she told her about her decision almost made it impossible to breathe. Kylee blinked away threatening tears. She needed to get back to the city, holidays or not. She'd had her time with the twins, and it had proved she wasn't meant to raise them. Her life was in New York, not theirs. Wouldn't Evan be relieved?

Finally, she heard the familiar knocking on the front door and slid out of bed. She made it to the hallway just as Evan was letting himself in. He looked nice in dark jeans and a soft flannel shirt over a fitted T-shirt, and her heart skipped. When she walked into the living room, she could smell the scent of the outdoors mingled with something uniquely Evan. It made her palms dampen.

He studied her, oblivious to her attraction as Mom rose to her feet. "I was just heading back home," her mother said. She glanced back at the couch where Henry had drifted off. Music played softly from the television tuned to a holiday channel.

"Oh, okay," said Kylee, trying to shake off her feelings for the man with his hands in his pockets. "Annabelle's still asleep, too."

Mom smiled. "I forgot to tell you I brought a loaf of cranberry bread from The Last Re-Torte. It's in the pantry."

Kylee's mouth watered. "Thanks, Mom. You'll be back tomorrow then?"

"The children are fine. You call if you need me."

"Thank you, Mrs. Spokes," said Evan. "For everything you've done."

"Of course. These are my grandchildren."

"We couldn't have done it without you," insisted Kylee.

"Oh yes, you could have," insisted the older woman. She gave Evan a long look, then turned to Kylee. "You two make a great team. Your sister knew what she was doing." Mom twisted to look at the blinking Christmas tree. "And so does God. Just keep doing what you're doing, and our family will be okay."

Evan gave a small chuckle that sounded more polite than sincere, and Kylee struggled for something to say, knowing this was not the time. She couldn't bear to see Mom's disappointment over her leaving again. Instead, she walked to the coat hooks beside the front door and helped her into a thick wool cardigan Kylee had bought for her years ago in Ireland. "Are you sure you're okay to drive?" Kylee asked in concern.

"Oh yes. It's just three miles, you know."

"Well, if you ever want me to pick you up, you just have to call," insisted Evan.

Kylee watched the exchange with a warm heart. This man was as kind to her mother as he was to her and the twins. There wasn't an unfriendly bone in his body.

Mom clutched her purse and stepped out onto the porch, but then she turned back. "What is it they say? The trees are about to show us how beautiful it is to let things go? I let go, I let God, and I do the best I can."

Kylee smiled at Evan when he shut the door and turned around.

"She's a gem," he said.

"Always has been," Kylee assured him.

"I'm glad she's able to help out, even with her health issues."

"Yes, but it's hard on her," Kylee admitted. "I see that now."

He stood with his arms crossed over his chest as if he didn't mean to stay.

She swallowed. The twins were asleep, and she and Evan were alone. Now was the time. "Um, Evan, there's something I wanted to talk about."

"Okay. Me, too, actually."

She motioned toward the kitchen table after remembering that Henry was snoozing in the living room. Evan followed, and she pulled out a chair for him, then drifted over to the counter to start the electric teakettle.

She tried to organize her thoughts, plan her words. She had her excuses, but she hadn't considered how to explain them. When she returned to the table with mugs, he rose up as if they were at a formal dinner and took them. She sat down, mildly embarrassed at his manners. He looked gorgeous and smelled achingly wonderful. He would be the perfect father to the twins. The pain of letting all of this go—the cottage, the memories of her sister and the beautiful young lives planted here—was gutting. She put a hand to her throat.

He stared.

"You go first," Kylee blurted, wanting to put it all off.

He studied her. "No, I…" His gaze shifted toward the luggage set near the door. "You all are packed, I see."

"Almost, but…" Kylee took a breath. "The thing is, I've decided to let the twins stay for the Nativity."

"Are you serious?" Evan's eyes widened with surprise. "That's so kind of you. I—I mean, they'll love it, and everyone will be happy to see them before they go." He glanced at the suitcases again. "So you changed your flight?"

"That's just it," admitted Kylee. "I'm going to let them stay. Here."

Amazement lit up Evan's face, and he smiled. "Kylee, that's wonderful!" he said, almost laughing with happiness. "I knew you'd come around. Who can resist the great city of Lagrasse? Everyone is glad you're home, and everyone loves—you," he stammered.

She tried to smile but couldn't, and he became serious.

"I care about you, you know. I'll always be here, always be your friend." He took a deep breath. "At the least."

The words tacked onto the end of his declaration bumped off the ceiling and rained back down on her. *At least?* He was one in a million, but she was not his type and didn't deserve him.

"No," she said, heart thudding so hard it turned her stomach over. "That's not what I meant."

The gurgling kettle clicked off loudly in the silence. Evan gaped, his faint smile melting like snow in the sunshine.

"I mean the twins are staying here, and I'm going back to New York for Christmas alone," said Kylee. "To stay." Before he could reply, she insisted, "I tried to tell you at the hospital. You really are the best choice for the children. They need to stay here. With you."

Evan stared at her like she'd stolen something from him. "Kylee, I... I'm not even sure what I'm going to do with my life right now. I mean, I'm not cut out to be a paramedic." He motioned down the hall where Annabelle slept. "She's hurt because of me. You're a better parent."

"What are you talking about?" exclaimed Kylee in exasperation. "You're amazing."

Evan's eyes darkened like the shadows outside. "How can you say that after..."

"You're still blaming yourself for Chip and Mia?" Kylee sighed.

"That's the pot calling the kettle black. You belong here," Evan returned. "Mia loved *you.*"

Kylee blinked and looked out the window to avoid letting Evan see into her soul. "I wish I could believe that."

"You're going to have to believe it. They need you. If

I quit my job, I'll be moving out of town and back to my family farm."

Kylee's heart dropped. "They need to be raised in this house for now. Pulling another rug out from beneath them might break them."

"And that's why you have to stay."

She shook her head. "I can't, Evan. This is why I think with my head instead of my heart. I just…can't."

"*You* have the love they need." He looked so intently at her, she wondered if he was thinking of something else to say. "*You* are so much more than you think you are," he whispered.

How could the twins need her love when her sister hadn't? Kylee scooted back from the table. Fleeing to Mia's room, she clicked the door shut softly behind her so as not to wake the twins and leaned against it to keep Evan out. Tears slid down her cheeks, hot from the rapid thrashing of her heart.

Minutes later, she heard him moving around in the kitchen, and unable to face him again, grabbed a sweater and hurried down the hall and out the front door as if on an important errand. She didn't say goodbye.

On Monday, the temperature plummeted unexpectedly, and a social worker called Evan to request a meeting. Evan knew that meant Kylee was really going to go through with it. She was giving up custody.

He hadn't seen her or the twins at church on Sunday. Mrs. Spokes had explained Kylee wanted to keep Anna-belle home to rest. It made sense, but he knew the real reason behind it. She didn't want to have another conversation because she had no intention of changing her mind.

She'd bailed on her family, her sister and now her niece and nephew. He should have never let himself believe she was anything different than what he first assumed. She'd convinced him that she would put everything in order, but instead, she was abandoning the children and her hometown.

And she'd crushed his heart, too.

Evan started packing up his apartment, knowing he needed to give the Lightfoots some notice, whether he moved to the cottage with the twins or back home. If he was made responsible for them, he would only be able to work part-time. But where? His gut twisted with anxiety. Seesawing between frustration and numbness, he dressed slowly, then picked up his things to head to work.

When he walked into the warmth of the firehouse kitchen, there appeared to be a meeting at the table. His coworkers were gathered around it with sheets of paper and newspaper clippings.

"Here's the man of the hour," remarked Chase.

Evan slanted his head, then darted a look at James. Hadn't he told them Evan would not be accepting the promotion?

His captain pushed out a chair. "Have a seat."

Evan gave him a suspicious look and surveyed the men and women seated around the table. All eyes were on him. "What's going on?"

"We were just reminiscing," said James.

"About what?" Evan dropped into a chair. He picked up the nearest newspaper and scanned it. His first call. Twelve years ago. He'd actually been a ride-along, but he'd helped rescue a dog from a drain pipe. The owner, a retired veteran, had clutched the filthy wet terrier and propped his arm over Evan's shoulders as if they were best buddies for a picture. Evan looked up from the clipping and found Chase grinning. "What's this?"

"We were just discussing the new lieutenant."

Evan shot a questioning stare at James.

James put his elbows on the table and clasped his hands together. "Did you know in the last twelve years you have calmed, treated or saved over fifteen hundred people?" Evan started to protest the astounding number, but his boss interrupted him. "Remember the Baylors?"

Shawna pushed a report across the table. The Baylors had nearly died in their beds during an enormous house fire. They thought the newly retired couple had passed away, but Evan had felt in his gut that there was still a chance for both of them and insisted on CPR all the way to the hospital. Mr. and Mrs. Baylor revived and eventually recovered without any major problems. "That was God's doing, not mine," said Evan.

"You were His hands," said James. "Look, everyone agrees you're the best man for the job, and you've been here longest. We know you have a lot on your plate with the twins, but if anyone can manage it, you can with that gal of yours."

"She's not my gal. Kylee's leaving town, and she's decided not to keep custody of the children," Evan said. "Even with their grandma's help, I'll be the one responsible for them, and you know what happened with Chip and Mia." He climbed to his feet. "I panicked that night. I could have done better. Maybe one of them would have survived."

"Wait a minute." Shawna held up a hand, her dark eyes blazing. "If you hadn't felt any regret after that, I'd be worried about you." She frowned. "Doing your job is one thing, but when you're holding family or friends in your arms, it's personal. What makes you think you're supposed to be some kind of miracle worker? Few people could have survived that accident even if they were life-flighted out."

"You just said I was His hands."

"But you're not His decision-maker. Do you think Chip would have wanted you to throw in the towel on your dreams just because his life was over?"

It was a cliché argument, but that didn't change the answer. Evan exhaled in frustration, but his coworkers weren't finished.

James leaned forward. "Have you ever stopped to think that you being there was a gift? I'm sure it gave them peace knowing you would take care of things. That's why you were there."

Evan's throat pinched, and his eyes watered. He studied the kitchen counter, unable to meet anyone's eyes.

"You are a brilliant paramedic, Evan, and you're a wonderful godfather," insisted James. "The kids couldn't ask for anything more and neither could our community. No one expects you to give up this job because there were people you weren't able to save. Give yourself a break."

"We can't save everyone," Shawna reminded him. "But that sure doesn't mean we stop trying or caring."

Evan glanced at the scattered reports and clippings all over the table. He had done a lot of good despite the failures. But what about the twins? "That doesn't mean I can be a parent," he said. "If something happened to one of them on my watch..."

James gave Evan a piercing look. "Evan, my son died because he made a foolish decision. Did I talk to him enough about drinking? Probably not. Did I let consequences slide and fix his problems for him? Too often. I was responsible for him, but that doesn't mean I'm responsible for his death. He made a choice, and God decided to take him home. I couldn't live his life for him—or anyone else."

"No one is fireproof," Chase piped up with a serious expression. "We do the best we can. The twins won't be any safer with someone else than they would be with you. Certainly not me," he joked.

Evan had a sudden image of Chase feeding the twins fast food in a messy room in front of a TV with a video game on the screen. He laughed. "I'll have to agree with you there."

"See?" James took a deep breath. "So does anyone have a problem with our new lieutenant?"

Everyone smiled and shook their heads.

James scraped back in his chair loudly and lumbered to his feet. He circled the table and offered Evan his hand. "Congratulations, Lieutenant Hollister."

The handshake was warm, but even as a peaceful assurance flowed through him, Evan knew without the twins, and someone like Kylee, he'd never have it all.

Chapter Fifteen

It felt like a funeral in the house on Tuesday morning. Mom had taken the news hard the day before but came over anyway. Annabelle wailed from her bedroom. Henry sat listlessly on his mother's bed watching Kylee pack as the sun rose. She zipped up the last suitcase just as Mom walked into the room. Kylee heard her tired and disappointed exhale. Ignoring her, Kylee moved the bag to the floor, scooped up Henry and sat down. He clutched her arms with his small hands.

"Tam will check in once a day," promised Kylee. She looked around the near-empty bedroom she had moved her things into after the charity truck came. "She said she didn't mind until Ali can work things out to start babysitting."

"It's nice of her to take over babysitting until they start school next year," Mom admitted. "I know the extra income will help with the new baby."

"See? It's all worked out," said Kylee.

"But Evan…" Mom began.

Kylee flinched. He hadn't been over since she'd told him she would surrender custody. It was like he didn't want to see her. As if her leaving wasn't a big deal. But she knew it was. He was upset at her for not taking the twins, but someday he'd see this was best. "Evan will come over tonight,"

Kylee informed her. "The Nativity program is tomorrow—Christmas Eve. They really need the twins. I know you need to check on Uncle Tim, so he'll take them."

"I'm Joseph," said Henry.

"I know." Kylee gave him a loving squeeze. "I'm so proud of you for being in the play."

He turned around. "I'm not going to play, I'm going to behave. I'm going to take care of Jesus's family."

Kylee's eyes misted. "And you're going to do a great job."

"Annabelle will, too," he added. He wiggled down and left the room in search of his sister.

Mom sat down on the bed beside her. "Are you sure about this, honey?"

"I'm sure."

"I loved having you home, Kylee. Everyone's going to miss you, and I'm going to miss our talks." Kylee stared at the floor until her mother leaned closer. "You know that right? You have always been missed—and loved."

Sudden tears trickled down Kylee's cheeks. She brushed them away. "I wasn't always here when I should have been."

"And why was that?"

Kylee remained silent, then gathered her courage. "I just never thought I fit in or was useful."

"You do fit in. And you're needed now."

"Evan will do a better job than me," Kylee insisted. "Look at all he's done."

"He did it with you. He didn't *outdo* you."

Kylee bit her lip. Her mother wasn't wrong. They did make a good team, but…it was impossible. In the end, she wasn't what the children needed, and besides, she had feelings for Evan, and they would get in the way like a bad office romance. "I have to get back to New York," she blustered. "They need me at work." She gave her mother a wry smile. "I've been informed I'm getting a bonus."

Mom didn't congratulate her. Instead she said, "If that's what fulfills you, Kylee."

"It's all I know how to do."

"I have to disagree."

"I'll never be Mia, Mom," said Kylee.

"I never expected you to be. We didn't need two of the same person. You were always a great help to me, and your father couldn't get himself to work and back without your help, much less the doctors when he was sick. You got things done."

Kylee glanced at her. "It's nice to know I was appreciated."

Her mother sighed. "Your pictures were plastered all over the house right beside your sister's, and your father couldn't let a Sunday dinner pass without telling everyone what you were doing in New York. Mia was always asking if we'd seen your photos online—the office, your apartment, and when you were interviewed by that fancy magazine."

"I didn't know that," said Kylee.

"We weren't good at handing out praise like we should have," admitted Mom.

"I'm not very good at it, either," admitted Kylee. She rose to her feet. "I should thank Evan, you know. Before I leave."

"He's not coming over until later."

"Oh. That's right." Kylee smiled to hide the fact that the reminder tied her stomach in knots. "I guess I could go make the twins some breakfast."

Mom wagged her chin. "Good luck. Annabelle is under the bed and refuses to come out until you bring Charlotte back to life for Wilbur."

* * *

Later, after a quick meal, Kylee hugged her mother, then forced herself to tell the twins goodbye, bracing herself for Annabelle's tantrum. Instead, the little girl was eerily quiet, lying on the couch beside her brother and only accepting a limp embrace.

Henry threw himself into Kylee's lap. "When can I come and see the ice skates and gingerbread men?"

"Maybe next year," said Kylee. She squeezed him tight. "I'll be back at Easter, and we'll video chat every Sunday, okay?"

"Okay, but what about dinosaurs?"

"You'll have to play with Evan until I get back."

Henry looked up with bright eyes. "He isn't very scary," he informed her.

Kylee laughed. "Are you saying I am?"

"You're the best fighter," he said. "But you never hurt me."

"Because I love you."

"I love you, too," Henry declared.

Kylee glanced at Annabelle. The little girl scowled. "I'll be back soon, Annabelle, and you can have Evan or Nanna call me whenever you need to talk."

"Don't. Go," retorted Annabelle in two sharp syllables.

"I have to get back to my office," said Kylee. "You'll be fine."

"No, I won't," the little girl warned, and Kylee's heart stung.

She searched for something to say, but her mind—and heart—were empty. A part of her knew the children wanted her, but someday they would understand.

Mom stared at the news on TV with fatigue etched into her face.

"Evan will be here soon," Kylee promised. "I'll call when I get in."

"Okay, sweetheart," her mother said.

"Don't forget they have a playgroup activity next week at the children's museum."

"I won't. I'll take them if I can," Mom assured her.

"Don't stress yourself. Ali will drive them on days you don't feel up to it, and remember, Saturdays we go to the bookstore."

"Yes, I know, you put it on the calendar."

Kylee tugged at the luggage beside the front door, knowing she was dawdling. "Annabelle isn't allowed to touch any of the books unless a grown-up is holding her hand."

"That's a very good rule."

"And don't let her in the tree behind the hammocks."

"I know." Mom climbed to her feet and walked over with her arms outstretched. Kylee met her for another embrace.

"She likes to climb things. Oh!" Kylee put a hand to her chest. "They're starting a pre-K program at the church next summer. I applied for them. They really need to get their feet wet before kindergarten. I'll forward you the email as soon as I hear anything."

Mom frowned. "You might as well call me, honey. I don't read those very often."

"Right, right." Kylee's heart began to thrum. Why was turning over the reins so difficult? She gave her mother a final hug when the taxi pulled up outside. She paused at the door, deliberating on whether or not to call out to the twins, who'd disappeared. No, they'd said their goodbyes. It wasn't like they were hanging on her legs trying to drag her back inside.

She took a deep breath and stepped out of the house, just as Mom called, "Kylee?"

She looked back.

"You know I'm proud of you, right?"

Kylee's cheeks warmed. "Of course."

"We've always been proud."

"Thanks, Mom." Kylee gave her a little wave, then headed toward her ride with fresh tears stinging her eyes.

First class. Window seat. Lap blanket. *Back to my life.* Kylee tried to relax as a dazzling night sky filled the airplane window, but she had no desire to recline or take a nap. The perks her airline points provided weren't enough to drown out a voice in her head. *If you're sure that's what you want. It's your decision.* They were words her parents always offered even when they were hurt or disagreed. *You do you.* It was the only way they knew how to love her, Kylee realized, so she'd learned to speak for herself and make all of her own decisions regardless of who she left in the dust.

"Would you like a snack?" interrupted a flight attendant.

Kylee smiled and shook her head. "Just some hot water. Tea, maybe?"

"Good choice," said the gracious woman. "It'll keep you warm until you get home to your family."

Kylee gave her a tight smile. "Is it snowing in New York?"

"Not that I know of," the attendant admitted. She moved on to the next passenger behind Kylee's seat.

Kylee sighed. No snow was waiting for her at home; just an apartment, which would be dark, cold and quiet— with *nothing stirring, not even a mouse*. She turned back to the window. Miles above the earth where time and space expanded, she thought she could detect the twinkle of Christmas lights below. The entire Christian world would celebrate the Savior's birth tomorrow night. The gift of all gifts. His life was always the answer. His way, the best way. She pressed her forehead against the window, looking for guidance in the atmosphere. Was she making the right decision?

The night sky was blue-black with rolling carpets of misty clouds. What would her life look like when it was all said and done? Mia had brought two babies into the world and was a light to everyone around her. And Evan watched over his family and friends. What did Kylee have to offer that truly mattered?

Nothing. Nobody would remember her job when she left this life, the brand of shoes she wore or the kind of purse she carried. No one would quote her address or pass around pictures of her elegant, chic apartment. In fact, people who would say anything about her were from home. Lagrasse.

Kylee's nerves tightened, and she shifted in her seat, fighting tears. She missed the kids, and she missed Evan. Her heart felt like a wilted flower. What would happen if Evan met someone? Fell in love? What would it be like to be loved by him—to be favored by him above all other women?

A twinkling star, bigger than all the rest, caught her attention outside the window. The North Star. It shimmered, extending rays of light to touch the earth below. It was a safe, guiding light for travelers on their way home. Its arms seemed to stretch past the airplane as if reaching back for Lagrasse. *This way*, it blinked. *Home.*

The twins. Evan. He'd been her North Star these past few months in the midst of all the turmoil. And she loved him. *You are so much more*, he'd said. She was more. And she'd used Mia as an excuse not to realize it. Success and its rewards had been all she cared about because she thought they would make others care about her.

But no one in Lagrasse cared about her salary, where she lived or how respected she was. They asked how she was doing or what they could do to help with the children. Her children. She could have brought the twins with her to New York, but she didn't want to. She wanted them to have a childhood in Lagrasse. That was the underlying truth beneath it all, whether she was worthy enough to raise them or not.

Kylee stared hard at her reflection in the cabin window. It was her sacrifice. Her gift to Mia, the twins and Evan. She enjoyed her job and the life she'd built all on her own. Choosing to leave Lagrasse and make it big had been scary, but she'd done it. It'd been hard. People had no idea how much she'd struggled. She was proud of herself. And now, she knew, her family was proud of her, too. She could rest assured the children would be safe and happy in the small town that had made her who she was—the place that held her heart.

The cold mist that hung over Lagrasse all day turned into a near-freezing sprinkle as the temperature dropped through the afternoon on Christmas Eve. By evening, the children were so excited they sprinted across the packed parking lot in their jackets, ignoring the damp and cold. Evan hurried to grab Henry by the collar. "Be careful," he warned him. "You could have gotten hit by a car."

"I looked," Henry protested, and he tugged away.

Evan let him go. He would have to let the little boy experience some consequences, but he couldn't resist adding, "Take your time. You could get hurt."

"Uh-uh," argued Annabelle. "It's Christmas." She hopped

onto the sidewalk and promptly tripped and fell to her knees. Evan sucked in a breath of concern, but she quickly jumped to her feet and looked down. "Ow."

"I told you so." Evan crouched to examine her legs for any bleeding, but she took a step back and pressed down her dress.

"I'm okay. I can still be Mary." Wincing, Annabelle walked slowly alongside her twin to the door on the side of the building that led into the Good Shepherd Church annex, and Evan followed them holding their costumes.

He was happy they were all together tonight, but he couldn't find the joy he knew he should feel. A part of them was missing, and that part was Kylee. He was more than grieving her loss; he was heartbroken.

But Annabelle was okay, he told himself. James and the crew had been right. Evan had to let the twins do things on their own; experience life and make their own mistakes. He couldn't jump in and play goalie every time he thought they might hurt themselves. He could only guide them; he couldn't lock them in the house for the rest of their lives. He had to trust himself, and he had to trust God. Evan swallowed a sour taste in his mouth. Even if that meant falling for a woman who might not feel the same way.

Kylee had made him a happier person. And she'd given him these beautiful children. The sadness that had threatened to squash him for days crept back up his spine, and he slumped as he let himself in the door.

A mouthwatering aroma of Christmas ham filled the hall, and Evan followed the twins into the annex, realizing he smelled scalloped potatoes, too. He eyed the festive red, green and silver decorations draped everywhere from floor to ceiling. Electric candles flickered on the tables like stars. When he turned to remark on them to Kylee, he remembered she wasn't beside him, and his heart crashed to the ground again.

Henry had climbed up at a table beside Tam and Piper. Evan lifted a hand in greeting as he approached. "Do you have room for three more?"

"We do." Tam scooted a chair out for him. She wore a very peculiar sweater with a pig in front of a barn decorated for Christmas.

"I see you dressed up," Evan noted with a raised brow.

"Ugly sweater contest." She grinned.

"Oh? First I've heard of it," Evan confessed as he slipped into the chair. Two servers from the youth group appeared and handed them all plates of food.

"Bread!" cried Annabelle in delight.

Evan almost smiled. At least she would eat something.

"How are they?" asked Tam, motioning toward the children.

Annabelle stuffed a roll in her mouth. "Please don't do that," Evan chided her. "You're going to choke." He sighed and turned back to Tam. "Their grandma went to Dothan until tomorrow. They're doing okay for the most part thanks to Kylee."

"Aunt Kylee said that's rude," said Henry.

Kylee *was* the most part, Evan wanted to add, but he took a bite of potatoes.

Annabelle giggled and set down her bread.

"Did Kylee make it home?" Tam asked.

Evan shrugged and hoped it looked nonchalant. "I guess. She left yesterday."

Tam slanted her head to the side. "Are *you* fine?"

He glanced at her, then found a spray of evergreen bough to study. "I'll survive."

"Of course you will. You're good at that." She gave him

a look of sympathy. She suspected, he realized. Had she known before he did?

"I, uh, yeah. I'm okay." But he was not. He pushed his plate away as another wave of misery washed over him, and he let his gaze wander the room bursting at the seams with joyful families. He didn't just miss Kylee. He was in love with her. Beside the stage, a tall Christmas tree was decorated with big red ornaments. A delicate crystal star rested at the top. A wish. A guide. A sign. His heart shuddered. The back-and-forth of his emotions was going to kill him, he thought in exasperation. Tonight was about the twins. It was Christmas.

"You two stay here with Tam," he instructed Henry and Annabelle. There were no complaints as they stuffed more rolls into their mouths. Evan went backstage and began pulling the stable forward to its position. The Nativity was supposed to start after dinner, but no one had begun to set up.

Monk joined him, brushing crumbs off a white dress shirt. He'd grown a lush silvery beard that made him look like a lumberjack.

"Are you playing Santa somewhere?" Evan joked.

Monk chuckled. "They asked me to at the elementary school."

"That's fun," said Evan. "And I was only teasing."

"It's nice to be included at my age," admitted Monk. "And it makes the youngsters happy."

"That's what Christmas is all about." Evan searched the other side of the room. Children were tugging on their parents because it was time to put on their costumes.

As Monk secured the stable to the floor, Evan went back for the stable's star. Clutching it in his hands, he realized how delicate life could be, and love, too. It was a sign—

of the Word that would save them all. The Savior was the true rescuer. The true shepherd. If only… Evan exhaled as he returned to the stage. It would be his mistake to fall for a woman who didn't want a family, who didn't want the twins…or him.

What little dinner he'd eaten sank to the bottom of his stomach. For now, the twins would just have to be content with a godfather. He only wished he had someone at his side. Someone who cared for him and could offer him comfort for a change. But as life would have it, Kylee was not in love with him. She'd given it all up. She'd said it was all for the twins, and he tried his best to believe that she meant it.

Children began wandering to the stage at Sister Lovell's command. Evan felt a tug on his pants and looked down.

Annabelle held up her bathrobe with a pout. "I need to put my costume on."

"Oh, yes." Evan's heart skipped a beat as he realized people were beginning to throw away their paper plates. He crouched down beside the manger and helped Annabelle into her robe, then tied a piece of fabric over her head as her head covering.

Without further instruction, she knelt solemnly at the manger and reached in to pat a doll bundled in strips of torn gauze. "This is my family," she murmured, and the words—repeated countless times through the ages—pierced his heart.

Family, he thought. It was time to stop worrying about whether or not he was worthy. He reached down and squeezed Annabelle's shoulder as shepherds and sheep began to crowd around them. "Where's Henry?" Evan whispered, realizing a member of their family was missing.

"He's getting his costume on," replied Annabelle.

"Where?"

"I don't know."

I don't know meant Annabelle wasn't concerned or interested. She gazed out over the audience that was beginning to quiet, reverent in a way he'd never seen her before. Christmas had come to Lagrasse.

Evan ducked off the stage, scanned the room, then let himself out into the hall. He checked the bathroom, then the sanctuary. Concerned, his pace quickened, and he tried to tamp down any sense of panic. Why had he let Henry out of his sight? He hurried back into the activity hall and rushed to the table where they'd eaten dinner.

Tam was leaning back in her chair, talking to Angie Coles at the next table.

"Tam!" He realized his voice was raised. "Where's Henry?"

"They didn't find you?" She smiled at him and something twinkled in her eyes. "Back there." She pointed.

In an alcove at the back of the room, where tables and chairs were usually stored, Henry stood as still as a statue with his arms at his sides. With him stood Kylee, tying a bandanna across his forehead to keep a piece of fabric draped over his head. She was wearing a dark red sweater and black slacks.

Evan's heart rose with joy—and relief. She'd come back! But why? He'd wanted to beg her to stay but had been too afraid to tell her why. It was more than for the twins. More than for sharing responsibilities. His nerves tightened. Taking a deep breath, Evan wove his way toward them through the settling crowd.

Henry looked up and grinned at him.

"They're about to start," Evan said in a strangled voice.

Kylee didn't miss a beat. "There." She dropped her hands from Henry's head. "You look smart and handsome."

"But do I look like Joseph?" Henry demanded.

"I think you look just like what he may have looked like." She patted him on the head, and Evan wondered if she was avoiding his gaze. "You look like your dad," Kylee whispered.

"Hurry on up there, Henry. Annabelle's waiting," said Evan, his voice thick and heavy. The boy dashed away, and Evan held his breath as Kylee turned to face him. Her hair was pulled up off her long neck. Diamond studs sparkled in her earlobes. Evan let his gaze wander across her smooth cheeks before he met her eyes. They were dark and hypnotic in the dim lighting, watchful despite her cheerful greeting.

"You don't look surprised to see me." Her voice was husky, as if she was running on little sleep.

"I thought you were in New York."

"I was. I got in last night." She stared at him with a small smile.

"And yet here you are," said Evan, confused.

"That's right."

"So…" He was unsure what to say. "You're back for the Nativity?"

"I realized I needed to be here and got right back on the first flight this morning."

He was speechless, unable to get any words out of his mouth.

"I hoped we could talk," she began.

Heart skipping, Evan replied, "About what?"

"The twins were given to me. They're Mia's greatest gift, and I realized that I was rejecting them by going back to New York. They need their aunt." She took another breath and swallowed, then said, "My decision was too hasty, Evan. I—I know I need to use my heart instead of my head sometimes. I'm supposed to be here. I…" She glanced toward the stage. "I belong."

Evan's heart was suddenly in his throat. Was she taking them back? "You belong with the twins?" he clarified.

She nodded. "And you," she added.

What could that mean? "You want to raise the twins together?"

"Yes," she said, and more relief lifted some of the weight off of his shoulders.

Another hope lingered. "We'll do this together then," he said.

"Yes." She smiled and exhaled. "Since the paperwork hasn't gone through, I don't see any reason for things to change."

"So you're going to keep custody."

"That's the plan," she said firmly, but her eyes softened, and she looked away. "Unless you ever decide you want to discuss joint custody."

"We couldn't do that," he began, then realized she looked anxious. Suddenly his heart soared from his chest. "I mean, we'd have to be a couple." He tried not to stumble over his words.

She gave a sharp, silent nod.

Evan wrinkled his forehead to keep his Christmas wish from tumbling out of his mouth.

Kylee cleared her throat. "Yes, it's always an option down the road, if—if—" He was certain her blush matched his. "You see, I love my family," she explained, "and it's time I show it. But I also care about… I mean, I—"

Evan felt amusement bubble up in his chest from out of nowhere. She was as cautious as he was but much more courageous. He took a deep breath. "Hey, that sounds great, and I'm glad you're back, but between you and me…" He drew a breath, willing it to give him more bravery than he'd had in a very long time. "Kylee, you should probably know I love you."

She stared at him as if dumbfounded.

He held his breath. Just to have her care about him would be enough, but he had to take a chance even if he failed.

To his surprise, she took a step forward and stopped inches away from him, making his stomach dance even more.

"Evan," she said, voice trembling, "I just quit my job and listed my apartment. I gave up everything…to come home for Christmas and stay." She paused for a moment. "I couldn't spend another day in New York without Henry or Annabelle. Or you."

Evan put a hand to his chest. "Me?"

"I like you, too," she said, then her eyes glimmered, and she looked down. "I mean, I love you, Evan," she admitted, voice breaking. "And I'll stay no matter what you decide. I'm here for the twins. But I'm here for you, too."

"When I asked you to stay, it wasn't just for the twins," Evan admitted. "It was for you. For you and me." Arrows of joy made him want to laugh and cry at the same time. He wrapped an arm around her waist and pulled her to him.

"When they had heard the king, they departed. And, lo, the star, which they saw in the east, went before them, till it came and stood over where the young child was," interrupted a voice over the loudspeakers.

Evan jumped, and Kylee chuckled. She dabbed at the corner of her eye. He waited for her to meet his searching gaze and found her open and vulnerable.

"When they saw the star, they rejoiced with exceeding great joy."

Angelic voices filled the air as the children began to sing.

Startled once again, Evan followed Kylee's stare toward the stage. Annabelle and Henry were holding hands and bowing reverently behind the manger. Henry looked solemn, and Annabelle beamed. Her small white teeth shone as bright as the star over their heads framed by evergreen boughs and mistletoe.

Evan's heart pounded in his ears. His soul overflowed with so much warmth. He released Kylee's waist and grabbed her hand. When she looked at him in surprise, he nodded his head toward the door and guided her out the back of the room. Thankfully, the hall was quiet and empty.

"What are we doing?" whispered Kylee, squeezing his hand.

Evan took a deep breath. "The program is almost over. We won't be missed. So I'm looking for mistletoe."

Kylee giggled softly and tugged his arm until she pulled him to a stop in the middle of the lobby. Headlights flashed through a window in the night's sparkling rain. Evan met her eyes and found them dancing. She reached into a pocket and pulled out a twig of greenery. "What's that?"

She flushed. "Mistletoe."

"Really?"

"Evan Hollister, you know I always come prepared."

He laughed and pulled her closer until her nose brushed his chin. "Hey, I'm taller."

"I left my heels in New York."

"Good," Evan cheered. "Because I like being able to lean over…" He touched her lips with his. "Merry Christmas, Kylee," he whispered as his heart bubbled over with happiness.

Her eyes glimmered. "Merry Christmas, Evan." Her eyes flicked over his shoulder, and he looked. The rain was sludgy now, turning to ice as the night deepened.

"We may have snow," he said in disbelief.

She put a hand on his cheek and kissed him again. "I brought it with me from New York."

Evan closed his eyes and felt love and hope, a future of happiness and the beginning of the family he'd been waiting for all his life.

Epilogue

Eighteen months later...

The Last Re-Torte Bakery still had its original historic brick facade, but inside, there were new pink walls and turquoise accents. Blown-glass light fixtures complete with curlicues looked like spun sugar, and glass cases displayed bread like fine art. Even the air seemed sweet, something Kylee Hollister appreciated as she repositioned herself on the cushion she'd brought along. She was always hungry these days, but the fragrance of cakes and pastries made her feel like she was starving.

The bakery's small party room was festooned with white, cream and lavender balloons. Kylee smiled as Evan handed her a second plate stacked with veggies and fruit. She thanked him and popped a grape into her mouth.

"Are you ready for this?" he whispered.

"Of course," she assured him. "I'm always ready." The truth was she'd felt off balance for the past few weeks, but Tam and Ali had assured her this was normal. Kylee gave her husband a penetrating stare. "The question is, are you ready, Captain Hollister?"

Evan winced at the new title he felt he'd earned too

quickly, but Henry jumped off the bench beside him. "Yes, he's a captain now like me." He grinned.

"That's right," said Kylee. "You're captain of the first and second grade bowling team, Henry, and Daddy Evan is captain of the firehouse."

Henry beamed at her.

"Do you think the baby will like the bowling alley, too?" Kylee patted her expanding tummy. "Being as it's almost the size of a bowling ball already, I'd say yes."

Henry giggled, but Evan wrapped an arm around her. "Healthy mothers make hearty babies," he said. "All we need is you safe."

"Is that supposed to make me feel better for showing early?"

"No," he admitted, "but that should." He pointed at the door.

Everyone cheered as bakery owner Donna Olsen appeared with a lavish white cake decorated with pansies and fern fronds and walked it to the table.

"Are we ready to eat?" asked Tam.

"That is absolutely gorgeous!" Ali exclaimed. She jumped to her feet as Donna set the cake carefully in the center. "I can't wait to see what it is."

"I hope it's chocolate!" exclaimed Annabelle. She was already seated by Kylee with a plastic fork in her hand.

"It can't be chocolate," Tam reminded her. She unwrapped a silver cake server with blue and pink ribbons tied to the handle and passed it to Kylee. Everyone stepped back, conversation dribbling to a stop. "This is a reveal party," said Tam. "If it's pink inside, it's a girl, and if it's blue, it's a boy."

Kylee put down her fruit plate and took a deep breath. She held out her hand to Evan. "Let's do it together."

"I want to help!" Annabelle exclaimed.

Henry cried, "Me, too!"

Realizing the momentousness of the occasion, Kylee gave Evan a quick nod. She stood up, and the four of them placed their hands on the cake server. "Boy or girl?" she teased while everyone held their breath.

"Boy!" shouted most of their friends.

"Girl!" cried the Coleses.

Kylee gave Evan a quick grin. "We already have a pair, so it doesn't matter to me."

"Me, either. Just you and our baby in good health." He brushed her cheek with a soft kiss.

She sent him a loving smile to say the words she could not say out loud with so much company surrounding them.

"Well, there can only be one me," Annabelle declared, interrupting the moment.

Kylee's eyes watered as she broke into nervous giggles.

"One!" shouted Tam.

"Two," joined in everyone else.

Kylee cut the cake on *three*. She felt her heart jump and tears brim at the first sight of pink crumbs. Within moments, cheers erupted around the room. Just as Evan clapped his hands with joy, Kylee reached the second layer. Then she exhaled, and sliced through the rest of the piece and held it up. Everyone stared, confused.

"It's pink *and* blue!" Annabelle roared. She looked at Donna standing at the door with a sheepish grin on her face. "Is it my brother or sister?" the little girl demanded.

Everyone turned to Donna, with no idea Kylee's heart was jumping hurdles in her chest. Donna gave a teasing shrug, her eyes locking with Kylee's gaze.

"I don't understand," Kylee stammered. "I thought it would be pink *or* blue."

"I had to make it both." The pastry chef grinned.

"Why?" said Evan, his tone steady but hinting at a frightening idea.

Kylee tried to put it together, her mind whirling. "The only way…"

"It's both!" Tam cried, throwing her arms in the air like someone had just scored a touchdown.

Murmurs echoed around the room. Donna covered her mouth and laughed. Kylee felt the blood drain from her face.

"That's impossible," Evan blurted.

"Not impossible," said Shawna with a shake of her head.

"This wasn't a mistake?" Kylee demanded.

"No, Madam PTA President," said the pastry chef. "You asked for a baby reveal, and this was the only way to do it. One boy. And one girl."

The room erupted into cries and laughter. Kylee felt her knees wobble and reached for the back of a chair, but Evan anticipated her needs. He pulled it out and helped her sit down, grinning so widely tears slid around the corners of his cheeks. "Kylee, I love you, but this is more than…" he began.

"You bargained for?" she finished, a hysterical laugh climbed up into her throat. Annabelle and Henry were jumping and shouting at her feet.

"I mean… I never dreamed we'd get—"

"Another set!" cried Tam.

Mrs. Spokes made her way through the crowd and gave Kylee and Evan a warm hug.

"Two for the price of one," Evan's mother whispered from beside them with reverent joy. "What a blessing."

Evan wrapped his arms around Kylee and held her tight. "A blessing indeed."

Kylee blinked away a tear. "We do not need a bowling *team*," she declared.

He nuzzled her ear. "Why have four interns when you can have an entire league?"

"At forty years old?" Kylee chuckled.

"Why not?" insisted Evan. "You manage two just fine, and I love jumping in to rescue you whenever you call my name."

She grinned at him. "And I love you at my side."

Her guardian, husband and friend took her in his arms again and murmured in her ear, "Babies and interns or not, it's where I plan to stay."

* * * * *

Dear Reader,

Thank you for joining me in Lagrasse with Kylee, Evan and the twins. I love a homecoming story, but coming home for Christmas and making peace with the ghosts of your past is even more special. Moving on can bless us and, as it did in Kylee's case, open our hearts. We all leave home for various reasons, but I believe that in most cases, God brings us back to the ones we love and who love us.

It isn't a perfect world, and families aren't perfect, either, but Christmas is a wonderful time of year to focus on who and what are really important as we celebrate the birth of Him who was without spot.

I hope you enjoyed this holiday story and that it brought you peace, happiness and a chuckle or two. A big thank you to my editors and the staff at Love Inspired, and most importantly to you, for reading my books and for your support of inspirational romance.

Warmly,
Danielle Thorne

   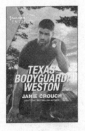